Ancient Magic

Dragon's Gift: The Huntress Book 1

Linsey Hall

DEDICATION

For Anne Nielson. A wonderful friend and inspiration.

PROLOGUE

Blood. I rubbed my tongue against the top of my mouth. Definitely blood. Fear shivered through me. The ground scratched my bare arms and the back of my neck. Prickly grass? My eyelids were gritty as I lifted them and blinked into the darkness. Stars twinkled down.

Night? Where was I?

Panic closed my throat. I gasped for air.

I pushed myself up and looked down. A ragged dress covered my skinny form, but didn't protect me from the chill night. I shivered as cold embraced me. A battered golden locket lay on my chest. It looked old, but I didn't recognize it.

A field stretched out around me, illuminated by starlight and a moon that hung low over the earth. The hair on my arms stood up at the sound of night creatures in the distance. A cold breeze rustled the grass, but fear chilled me more than the wind. Why was I out here?

Please don't let me be alone.

My heart thundered in my ears as I glanced around.

Two girls who looked to be about fourteen or fifteen lay sprawled on the ground beside me. They wore ragged dresses like mine.

Why was I here with two other girls my age?

Wait—were they my age? When I thought about it, I couldn't remember how old I was exactly. Just trying to think of it sent an icepick of pain through my skull.

With a trembling hand, I reached out and shook the girl closest to me.

"Wake up," I said. Panic sunk its claws into my chest. Why were we here?

When she didn't wake, I shouted, "Wake up!"

The girl gasped and shot upright, her black hair stuck with grass. Her terrified blue eyes met mine.

"Run," she gasped.

She spoke Irish, like I did, and the word shot straight through me.

"Hide," I said. "We have to hide."

I wasn't sure why, but I knew it more strongly than I knew anything else in the world. Her word—*run*—had triggered my own. *Hide.*

"Get up!" I scrambled to my feet. "We have to hide. Now. Now, now, now."

She clambered up, and we frantically tugged at the arms of the girl who still lay on her back. She was so pale she looked dead.

But I couldn't leave her. "Get up!"

She shrieked and jerked out of our hold, then crouched like a terrified animal. Her dark hair hung in her face.

What had happened to her, to us, that we were like this?

"FireSoul," she whispered, also in Irish. Her wide green gaze met mine through the curtain of hair.

The fear in her eyes must have mirrored my own. Her word pricked at my consciousness, but fear overrode it.

My heart pounded in my chest, trying to break my ribs. "Come on. We have to hide!"

She nodded and her head whipped around, searching for shelter like a cornered animal. I looked too. A small patch of woods about a hundred yards behind me caught my eye.

"This way." I spun and set off running across the field. They followed.

My lungs burned and my legs ached as we raced. I clearly wasn't used to being outside, nor to exercise.

But why? When I tried to think of the reason, nothing came but pain. My head ached when I tried to remember myself or my past. A sob burst from my chest. I couldn't remember anything.

Fear and the desperate need to hide drove me on when I wanted to stop and collapse to the ground, weeping. The trees loomed ahead—leafless, claw-like branches reaching for the sky. They were terrifying, but far better than the open field.

There was nowhere to hide in an open field.

Hide.

We dove into the woods, plowing through the underbrush until we were deep in the forest. Night creatures continued to rustle around us.

When we came to a large pile of collapsed trees, I plunged into them. Bark and branches scratched my arms as I found a nook created by the collapsed wood. The other girls crowded in behind me.

They were warm. Familiar, though I didn't recognize them. Safe.

We huddled together, panting. It wasn't quite as dark when they were near me, though it was more a feeling than reality.

Cold pinched my cheeks. I reached up and touched wetness.

Tears.

One of the other girls sniffled.

"What's your name?" I asked.

"It's—" The green-eyed girl started panting. Moonlight illuminated her panic-filled eyes. "I don't know!"

"I don't either!" the other girl cried. "I don't know my name!"

I tried to think of my own, poking for memories.

Pain.

I didn't know how old I was. Or where I was from. It hadn't been a fluke before. I really couldn't remember. "I don't know anything either!"

We gasped and cried, huddling closer. Their warmth felt familiar, like we'd done this a hundred times before. Slowly, it soothed me. I tried reaching into my mind to draw out some memories.

"Ouch." I cringed.

"What's wrong?" asked the dark-haired girl.

"Every time I try to remember something, my head hurts."

"Me too," said the green-eyed girl.

"And me," sniffled the other.

"Then what do we remember?"

"Run," said the dark-haired girl. "We're running, but I don't know from what."

"Is that how we got into the field?" I asked.

"Maybe." Her voice shook. "*Run* was all I remembered. When I woke, it was the only thing in my mind."

"*Hide*," I said, thinking back. "That's what I remembered. We must hide. From a bad man." I rubbed my temple. "Or woman? From someone very bad."

Just the shadowy memory made tears pour down my face. My shoulders shook. The trembling traveled down my arms and legs until my entire body quaked.

I couldn't remember who we were hiding from, but my body remembered. Hiding from evil. Bad. *Bad, bad, bad.*

The green-eyed girl threw her arms around me. "Hey, hey, calm down. It'll be okay."

I gasped through my sobs and realized I'd been saying *bad* out loud. I didn't believe that it'd be okay— not really—but her words made me feel a little better.

"What do you remember?" I asked.

"FireSoul," she whispered. "We are FireSouls."

I gasped and jerked out of her arms. "No, we're not. We can't be."

I might not have remembered my own past, but some knowledge of the world still seemed to be intact.

FireSouls were bad. Even the word sent a shiver of panic through me.

Run, *hide*, and *FireSoul* were my only memories? That couldn't be. In my mind, I poked for the biggest, most important pieces of information. I wanted to know something.

What came was that I lived in a world full of magic. Thoughts burst in my mind. "I'm one of the Magica—you two feel like Magica as well."

I could feel their power now that I tried. Could smell it and taste it. The green-eyed girl's power felt like water on my skin and smelled like flowers. Tasted like vanilla. The dark-haired girl was just as powerful. Her magic felt like soft grass beneath my feet and smelled like fresh laundry. It tasted sweet, but I couldn't place it.

"Magica?" the dark-haired girl asked.

"Magica can create magic!" the green-eyed girl said, excitement in her voice. "I remember now. But I don't remember what kind I am. Witch, or sorcerer, or... mage."

"Or shifter, demon, or fairy," I added as the memories flowed back. "But they aren't Magica. They are supernaturals like us, but they don't use magic the same way we do. But they know about us. Unlike humans. The Great Peace keeps us hidden." It came back to me in pieces. Though we lived alongside humans, the Great Peace—the most powerful bit of magic ever created—hid us from human eyes. It took the powerful spells of hundreds of Magica and shifters to create the Great Peace. "Humans can see us but not our magic, which we shouldn't use around them anyway."

"Right, I remember now," the dark-haired girl said.

"I feel your power too. But you don't feel evil," I said. "Not like a FireSoul would feel."

"We're not evil," the green-eyed girl said. "We haven't killed...I don't think. But I do remember that we're FireSouls. I know it."

"Everyone hates FireSouls," I whispered. They were the bogeyman because they stole the magical gifts of others by killing the original owner. Was *I* the bogeyman? Me and these two girls? Had I killed another Magica to steal his gift? Wouldn't I remember something as terrible as that?

"Is that why we're hiding?" the dark-haired girl asked. "Are we hiding from the Order of the Magica and the Alpha Council?"

"No," I said, though the two supernatural governing organizations would be after us if they knew we were FireSouls. "We're hiding from someone worse. But if we really are FireSouls, we can't tell anyone. They'll throw us in prison."

"We are FireSouls," she said. "When I woke, I knew it. It was my memory. As strong as yours."

I swallowed hard, remembering how strong that urge to hide had been. I'd woken confused, but when the dark-haired girl had said *run*, it had burst back into my consciousness.

"Are we really FireSouls?" the dark-haired girl asked. "I don't feel like a FireSoul. I don't feel evil."

I didn't either. I felt hungry and cold. My stomach growled and I shivered. If only I had something to eat. If only I was warm. I wanted it so badly.

A strange feeling tugged at my middle. As if there were a string tied around my waist that pulled me to the left. A sense of food and warmth flowed from the invisible string.

"There's food and shelter nearby," I said. "I feel it."

"Treasure," whispered the green-eyed girl. "You can sense treasure."

Treasure. Of course I could sense food and shelter. I coveted them. They were treasure to me right now.

I was a FireSoul. That was proof.

FireSouls were given that name because they shared a piece of a dragon's soul, though no one knew how it had happened. If dragons still existed, they were hiding. But legend said that all magic descended from dragons. FireSouls somehow shared a part of their soul.

That's why we could steal powers and find treasure. Dragons were covetous. They coveted treasure of all varieties—including the powers of others. The greatest treasure of all could only be obtained through death.

"We can find what we need with our dragon-sense," said the green-eyed girl. "If we want it badly enough, it becomes treasure. Then we follow our sense to it."

Was that how we were supposed to survive? Become hungry enough to find food and then steal it?

I looked down at my ragged dress and skinny body. The only thing I had of value was the necklace, and even that was probably almost worthless. It didn't look like I had a lot of choice right now. If I had parents, I had no idea who they were or how to find them.

My throat tightened. Did I have a mom and dad? Where were they? I pushed through the pain in my mind, trying to remember. But nothing came. Just blinding agony. I slumped against the other girls.

"Are you okay?" one asked.

"Yes." I pushed thoughts of parents away and focused on surviving. "If we use our dragon sense, we have to be careful."

If we were caught, we would be thrown in the Prison for Magical Miscreants. It was a cold, dark, terrible place, I remembered that. A shiver ran over me. My own personal bogeyman. In the corner of my mind, it felt like someone had once threatened me with that prison, but when I poked at the memory, the blinding pain came again. Why didn't I learn? I needed to quit poking at my personal past.

"We need names," I said.

"Yes. I hate not having one," said the dark-haired girl.

The green-eyed girl looked up at the sky. "I will be Phoenix. After the constellation. Call me Nix."

I liked that. Naming ourselves for something bigger gave me hope. I looked up too. A cluster of bright stars caught my eye. I didn't know what in my past had taught me the constellations, but I was grateful for it. "I'll be Cassiopeia. Call me Cass."

The green-eyed girl looked up and sighed. "You took the best ones."

I giggled, the sound surprising me.

"I'll take Delphinus," she said finally. "But it'll be Delphine. And you can call me Del."

"Okay. Del and Nix." They both looked so different. Panic gripped my throat as I realized that I didn't know what I looked like. I pulled my hair around. Red. "We look nothing alike. I don't think we're related by blood, even though we're all FireSouls."

They were rare from what I remembered, but I didn't recall the gift being genetic.

"We're sisters now," Nix said. "Because we're all we've got. I don't remember my parents."

"Me neither." Del sniffed back tears.

"We'll find them." I closed my eyes and focused on the idea of parents. I wanted them more than anything, so I should be able to find them.

But the magical string didn't tie itself around my middle. I thought harder, reaching into my mind, pretending it was a book I could flip through.

Agony pierced my skull.

I retreated, gasping.

"I tried to find them," I said. My parents were lost to me. My throat tightened and tears burned. "I don't think I know enough about them. I could imagine food and find that. But people are harder, I think."

"We'll find them somehow," Del said.

I nodded, trying to hope but finding it hard.

"We can only use our dragon sense to find food and other things we need," I said. "No killing for other powers." I didn't want to be a murderer, no matter how much power it got me.

Nix nodded. "I don't want to be a monster."

"Me neither," said Del.

"If another supernatural asks how we can find things, we say we are Seekers," I said.

The green-eyed girl smiled. "That's a good idea. Camouflage ourselves."

"Exactly." Seekers were a type of supernatural who could find things. As long as we didn't kill and steal powers, we could use our ability to find treasure and just say that we were Seekers.

"Do we have other powers we can use?" Del asked.

"I don't know," I said. If it was about me directly, I couldn't seem to remember. "FireSouls can be other types of supernaturals as well. You both feel magical to me."

Nix closed her eyes. I felt her power surge against me like water lapping at my skin. The taste of vanilla burst on my tongue, and her flower scent filled my nose. Her hands began to glow. She cupped them in front of her.

Eventually, a small match appeared in her palms.

"You're a conjurer," I said as my power swelled within me.

"Not a very good one," Nix said. "I wanted to conjure a fire for warmth."

I listened with half an ear as the power in my chest grew. It felt like it was in response to hers, spurred on by what she had. I embraced it, though I didn't understand it, and held my arms out. The magic pulsed within me, roaring to be released. I raised my palms to the sky and let it go.

An enormous fireball shot from my palms, throwing me back onto the ground as it roared into the sky. It burned away the tops of the trees and exploded into the night. Orange flames surged through the air, burning my skin.

Panic rose in my chest as I scrambled to my feet. We were trapped. Del and Nix looked at me with horrified eyes.

"I don't know what happened!" I said. The sky above me continued to burn, though the forest around us was untouched. "People will see the flame! We have to hide!"

Del lunged for me. She enveloped me in her arms and grabbed Nix, pulling her into the hug. A second later, the ground fell out from under me.

We collapsed to the ground a moment later. It was colder here, the wind stronger. I climbed to my feet. We were on a mountain looking down on the field below. Fire roiled in the air above it, a beacon of magic. But at least it wasn't lower. The animals and the people would be safe.

"We were in a valley," I said as I turned to Del. "And you can transport."

Del's wide eyes met mine. "Apparently. It was instinct. I followed it. And thank magic for it. What did you do down there?"

I looked down at the field that was lighting up the night. It would draw people. We were fine on the mountain for a little while because we were so far away, but we needed to get out of here soon.

"I didn't mean to light it all on fire," I said. "When Nix conjured the match, I felt like I could create a match too. So I let my power out."

"You're a Mirror Mage," Nix said. "You borrowed my conjuring power."

"A strong one," Del said.

"Too strong. I couldn't control it."

Mirror Mages weren't rare or very dangerous, from what I recalled. They could reflect back the magic of any supernatural that they were with. But it was just temporary, and the other supernatural got to keep their powers the whole time. From what I remembered, if Mirror Mages didn't use the borrowed gift right away, they could use it later. But it was a one shot deal. I could have held on to the conjuring gift I'd borrowed from Nix, but I'd only have been able to use it once.

In a way, Mirror Mages were a tiny bit like FireSouls because they used the powers of others. But they weren't very dangerous because they couldn't keep the magic or replicate it more than once.

I turned toward the valley. The fire was starting to dissipate, but it was still an unnatural spectacle, the sky alight with flame.

"I could have killed us if I hadn't pointed my hands to the sky," I whispered. "I'm dangerous."

"I think you need to practice," Del said.

"Or not use my power at all." Tears pricked at my eyes. Why was I like this?

"Let's not worry about that now," Nix said. "We should get out of here. Let's find food and shelter."

I nodded and blinked the tears away. "Okay. Let's go."

We set off along the mountain ridge, following the magical string tied around our waists. I was tired and scared, but at least I had my *deirfiúr*. My sisters.

But as I walked, the most horrible thought occurred to me. Had I been born a Mirror Mage, or had I killed someone for this gift?

CHAPTER ONE

Ten Years Later
Temple of Murreagh
Deep Beneath Western Ireland

"Cass! Answer me, damn it. Are you hurt?" Nix's voice echoed quietly from the pendant around my neck.

"Gimme a sec," I wheezed as I shoved the huge rock off my leg and scrambled behind a big boulder. Pain radiated from my shin, but nothing felt broken, thank magic. I didn't have time to deal with it anyway. A nasty looking shadow demon was currently trying to blow my head off. As long as my limbs were mostly functional, I was good to go.

A blast of magic blew apart the stone over my head.

I ducked and rubble bounced off my shoulders.

Damn demon!

When it stopped, I peered over the boulder at the demon who guarded the altar in the middle of the underground temple. It'd taken me nearly six hours to get through the enchantments that led to the temple. Fire charms, moving rocks, an awful riddle—the whole lot. Real Indiana Jones stuff, but I didn't have the cool hat.

After all that, it seemed like it should be smooth sailing. But no, this treasure was protected by a shadow demon. Who was apparently very displeased with my presence.

His skin was dark gray, his powerful body clad in simple pants and a shirt. He was basically human-shaped, except for the exceptionally bulky arms and the narrow black horns that came out near his temples and ran back along his skull. Dark eyes glinted maniacally through the dust in the air.

Though big, he was dwarfed by the subterranean temple that housed the Chalice of Youth, my current assignment. The chalice sat on an altar behind the demon, gleaming gold. Graceful columns supported the soaring stone ceiling, each carved in the shape of a different long-forgotten goddess. The only light came from eerie torches that lined the walls. The air was stagnant, permeated by the scent of smoke that wafted from the shadow demon.

"Do I send backup?" Nix asked through static.

"No. I've got this." I didn't usually need my friends to step in and save my butt on a job, but it gave me the warm fuzzies to know they were willing. "You're breaking up, Nix. Too much magic from the demon. I'm turning you off now."

Strong magic, like the kind the demon was throwing, usually interfered with the comms charm that hung around my neck. Something about the magical signature overpowering the puny charm that fueled my necklace.

I usually worked alone, but sometimes—okay, always—a riddle enchantment stumped me. At that point, Nix was there to back me up via a quick call through my comms charm. But now that she'd gotten me through the riddle that had opened the main door to this temple—Why does a dragon cross the road?—I no longer needed her help.

"Fine, don't—" More static broke up Nix's voice.

"If I'm not out in an hour, remember that I hate lilies," I said. "Worst funeral flower."

"But—"

I touched the silver charm around my throat, and its magic went dormant. Only the sound of the shadow demon's breathing echoed in the chamber.

It was time to get this over with. I was starving, and this was my last gig before the long weekend. My leg screamed as I pushed myself to my feet. *Breathe through the pain. It's just bruising.*

I drew my obsidian blades from the sheaths strapped to my thighs and stepped out from behind the boulder. Torchlight reflected wickedly off the black volcanic glass. Lefty and Righty, I called them—not nearly regal enough names for their power—but I'd never been good at clever names.

"Time to go back to hell, fella," my voice echoed in the stone chamber. "The devil says he's missin' ya."

The shadow demon laughed, his dark gray skin absorbing the light. Fine, it was a little corny, but I was tired.

The demon raised his hand to throw another blast of magic at me. I flung Righty at him, dodging the whoosh of magic that he managed to get off before my blade sunk into his arm.

Perfect hit. Ten points.

He roared in pain as heat seared my shoulder through my leather jacket.

Oh, so he wanted to play that way? With heat as well as wind? I thought wistfully of blasting him back with a reflection of his own power. His magic manifested as burning smoke. I'd give him a flaming tornado.

Except that was the problem. My magic was too powerful for me to control. I just blew shit up if I tried. I didn't want to draw attention to myself, so I didn't use my power. But I didn't hide that I was a Mirror Mage—strong supernaturals could tell I had magic. If I didn't use it often, my magical signature appeared weak to those strong enough to sense others' powers.

So I'd gotten really good with weapons.

I pricked the back of my hand with Lefty before immediately throwing the blade at the demon's heart. My blood ignited a spell that would call its twin back to me.

As Lefty hurtled toward the demon, Righty pulled itself out of the demon's arm and flew through the air toward me. As long as I was quick—which I usually was—I always had a dagger at hand.

I reached up and snagged Righty as I kept an eye on the dagger that zoomed toward the demon. He used magic to blast it away.

"That's all you've got?" he roared.

I dove behind the nearest column, a stone warrior woman in a flowing cloak, both of her hands gripping swords.

A guardian. Of me, I decided.

I swiped my dagger over the small amount of blood welling on the back of my hand so that my other blade returned to me.

The demon roared again, his muscles bulging beneath his thin shirt as he drew his arms back to throw twin blasts of magic at me. All supernaturals had different gifts and his seemed to be throwing blazing blasts of smoke that blew things apart like a grenade.

The smoke blast hit my guardian column. Her bottom half blew apart, rock and debris flying across the temple. With an enormous cracking sound, the guardian crashed to the ground. The stone floor vibrated beneath my feet. Dust filled the air until I could hardly see.

Guilt ate at me over the damage done to such an ancient place. Don't worry about that now. Fix it later. I jumped onto the guardian, who was now lying on the ground in several large pieces, all lined up in a row. I raced across her skirt, jumping from piece to piece until I was right above the shadow demon.

I leapt for him.

He looked up at the last moment, his eyes widening. He twisted and Lefty sank into his meaty shoulder. With a roar, he threw me off him. I skidded across the floor, then groped my way behind the top of the fallen column. He was strong, both in magic and form, and his magic smelled ancient. Like dust. I'd bet he was an old demon.

"Blades?" he yelled. "You come at me with blades? Use your magic and give me a real fight!"

"What? You bored? Been guarding this tomb a long time, eh?" I said as I flung Righty at him.

It sank into his chest, nearly a perfect shot at his heart. Or at least, where I figured a shadow demon's heart might be.

He yanked it out and said, "You have no idea."

I swallowed hard.

Missed his heart, I guess.

Quickly, before he could fling the dagger, I called it back to me. Righty pulled itself out of the demon's hand and flew home.

The demon didn't startle, nor did he look weakened by the dark blood leaking from the wound in his chest. Old and strong, like I'd thought. Even if I hadn't hit his heart, he should at least be incapacitated. But this one was different. He wasn't even winded from the blade that had sunk six inches into his chest.

"Well? Won't you give me a real fight? You are one of the three. Strong enough to fight, but you don't."

My heart tried to climb into my throat. "What does that mean?"

The three? Did he mean me and my *deirfiúr*? How could he know about Del and Nix?

"What do you mean?" I screamed when he didn't answer quickly enough.

"You don't use your powers." He threw another blast of magic at me. Blazing smoke blasted away my column barricade, and I scrambled back.

He wouldn't use his powers either if it meant getting locked up in the Prison for Magical Miscreants. As long as I didn't use them, I could pretend that I was nothing but a low-strength Mirror Mage and have a lovely life where no one tossed me in prison.

The shadow demon threw another blast of fiery smoke. It plowed into the ground in front of me. The stone floor exploded. The blast threw me backwards. Pain streaked through me. My entire front felt singed, pierced by small pieces of shattered stone. A cough tore through my lungs and I blinked blindly, my throat and eyes burning.

I could barely see, and he kept throwing those damned blasts of smoke at me, driving me ever backward. I just had to get him to lay off for a sec. Then I could question him.

Through the dust, I could make out his hulking form approaching. It was risky, but I threw each of my blades in quick succession, hoping to incapacitate but not kill.

The thud of a body collapsing sounded. The blasts of power stopped coming.

I climbed to my feet and limped toward the form sprawled on the ground. The stone bit into my knees when I dropped beside him. My blades protruded from his chest, one embedded in each pectoral. His breath strangled in and out of his lungs, but he wasn't dead. I grasped his rough shirt and shook him.

"What do you know about me?" I said.

"What"—he coughed—"you are."

"But—"

His lips parted, and I snapped my mouth shut, frantic to hear what he had to say.

"FireSoul."

I stumbled back, my stomach twisting. Chills raced over me. How could he know that? No one knew that but my *deirfiúr*.

"I'm a Mirror Mage." My voice came out hardly louder than a whisper. I tried again, louder, fear choking my throat. "I'm a Mirror Mage!"

Panic welled in me, and I crawled back to him, reaching for his shirt again, desperate to shake answers from him.

His eyes were dimming, their gleaming black light turning a dark gray. A great breath shuddered out of his lungs, followed by stillness.

The light faded from his eyes, and his body disappeared. My blades, no longer embedded in a chest, clattered to the floor.

"No!"

My heart threatened to break my ribs. I hit the ground, frustration and fear beating in my chest.

The demon was gone. Not dead—you couldn't really kill a demon—just send them back to whatever hell they'd originally come from. Normally very neat and tidy. Except this one had information about me, and my blades had been too accurate. The demon had seemed so strong when my first blade had found its mark. I'd wanted to question him more. This was what happened when I freaked out. Like a bull in a china shop. And it was the main reason I could never use my magic.

My breath echoed too loudly in my ears. Think, think. How could the demon have known that I was a FireSoul? Was it because this job was in Ireland, my homeland? At least, what I assumed was my homeland, given that I could speak Irish and had red hair.

One option was so terrifying I couldn't even poke it with my mind. It was the bogeyman that lurked at the corner of my memories. Whenever I pressed too hard, it leapt up, bringing with it a splitting headache and adrenaline like nobody would believe.

I had to get out of there. Talk to Nix.

Quickly, I grabbed my blades, shoved them into their sheaths, then climbed to my feet. I limped to the altar, pain singing up my leg, and grabbed the golden chalice. It's magic sang beneath my palm, an unsteady beat that indicated this was old magic. The perfect age for selling. There were other priceless objects too, no doubt tributes to the gods carved onto the columns.

My fingers itched to pocket a couple, namely a golden dagger encrusted with rubies and a strange hexagonal blade that looked wickedly sharp on all sides. Despite my terror, covetousness surged within me. My hand trembled as I reached toward the golden dagger. Just one touch. I wouldn't take it.

No.

I sucked in a deep breath and clenched my fist. Not mine. Not mine. Like an addict resisting a fix, I dragged my gaze away from the glitter.

With a shaking hand, I pulled a small black rock out of an inner jacket pocket. My last transport charm. Like all magic that wasn't my own, they were expensive and hard to come by. Del could make them because she could transport, but her power was limited and they commanded a lot of it, so she couldn't make them often.

I should use the charm only in emergencies.

But this sure felt like a heck of an emergency.

I threw the stone to the ground. It shattered and a glittering silver cloud rose in front of me. I stepped into the sparkling stuff and envisioned my home. Magic grabbed me around the waist and threw me through the ether.

CHAPTER TWO

By the time the portal spat me out in my little shop, some of my freak-out over the demon had faded.

Which was a good thing, because all hell had broken loose inside Ancient Magic, the entrepreneurial enterprise that kept our collective ship afloat. Del and Nix had been my besties since we'd woken in the field ten years ago. My *deirfiúr*.

"Nothing's ever simple, is it?" I muttered.

Two men with stupid black stockings over their heads were grappling with Nix in front of the counter. Looked like her afternoon had been just as adventurous as mine.

Despite their silly disguises, they were both huge, with hulking shoulders and ham-like fists. They'd each grabbed one of Nix's arms. Probably wanted to tie her up and rob the place. That was the usual deal.

I crossed my arms and leaned against the wall to watch. I'd step in if necessary, but I doubted it would be.

My *deirfiúr* and I had nicknames for each other. I was called Huntress because I hunted down the sparkles. Del was Seeker because she sought the artifacts we wanted in ancient texts and told me what to look for. And Nix was called Protector for damn good reason.

Quick as a blur, Nix jumped up and planted her feet on the chest of the thief to her right. She used his chest for leverage, kicking off and breaking his hold, then spun and kneed the other man in the chin so hard that he dropped to the floor, unconscious. She had to jump to do it, but she got good height.

I grinned as I watched her lay out the second guy with two kicks and a mean punch. He collapsed to the ground like a sack of boulders. I was grateful he didn't crush the table full of shiny things behind him.

But then, Nix was good at choosing where they landed.

She was taller than me, and though she didn't look any stronger, she was a heck of a lot better in a fistfight. Weapons were my game. My hand-to-hand skills were slightly better than good—enough to get me by on most jobs, which almost always involved sending a demon or two back to where they came from—but hers were almost preternatural.

She didn't look like she could kick someone's ass, though. She was dark haired and pretty, with warm green eyes and a big smile. Funky t-shirts and ripped jeans with motorcycle boots completed the picture.

"Nice job," I said.

Nix brushed her hands off and grinned at me. "All in a day's work. You get the chalice?"

I held it up. "Not my favorite job, but it's done. Let me help you with those guys."

Our shop was small. A narrow wooden counter stretched along one wall, shelves and tables on all the rest. Enchanted objects took up most of the space— everything from tiaras that would make a person beautiful to sleeping potions strong enough to rival the one that had knocked out Briar Rose.

Nix grabbed the enchanted cuffs off the counter and tossed me a pair.

I snagged them, then nodded at the counter where she'd had the cuffs waiting. We didn't usually keep handcuffs next to the register. Looked weird to customers. "Expecting these guys?"

"They weren't exactly subtle. I saw them crossing the street. No masks on yet, but all bulk and a walk like they kick puppies. Two and two equals robbery."

I nodded as I set the chalice on the counter, then bent to cuff the guy sprawled at my feet. I wasn't the only one who liked shiny objects, though these thieves were likely after the magic. Because of the value of the enchanted artifacts in our shop, there was a robbery attempt every few weeks.

After waking in the field ten years ago, we'd scrounged around for a living until we'd figured out how to profit from our skills. And thus Ancient Magic had been born. We found treasure imbued with ancient magic and sold it.

Ancient Magic was located on Factory Row in Magic's Bend, Oregon, but it was no Fifth Avenue. We provided our own security.

Magic's Bend was one of three all-magic cites in America that humans had no idea existed thanks to some powerful spells. Supernaturals lived in human cities as well, but this was one of the few places we could be ourselves. It made it the perfect place to set up a shop selling ancient magic.

While I was out hunting down enchanted artifacts, Nix manned the home front. It should have been an easy job—chat with customers, sell the goods, drink coffee from Potions & Pastilles next door. But of the three of us, she was the best at kicking ass and taking names, among other things. So she protected what I hunted. In addition to being Seeker, Del was a demon hunter the rest of the time, something that endeared us to the Order of the Magica, the government that ruled the Magica, and kept our shop on the good side of magical law. She was on a job right now, somewhere in South America.

I nudged the unconscious thief with my foot, then rolled him over so I could get at his back. It took some tugging, but I got his hands bound before I looked up to see Nix hanging up the phone.

She lowered the phone and glanced up. "Cops'll be here in a minute. Dispatch said there's a cruiser right around the corner."

"Good. Then we can grab something to eat. I'm starving." We'd had so many break-ins that Nix had become friends with most of the force.

It took only three minutes for the shiny police vehicle to pull up in front of the shop. Officers Cooper and Dale climbed out. It didn't take long for them to collect the thieves off our floor, or for Nix to give her statement. She was well versed by now.

Within ten minutes, they pulled away from the curb, criminals in tow.

"Glad that's over." Nix walked behind the counter and leaned on the wood, her brown gaze avid on the chalice. "So this is it? The Chalice of Youth?"

"The one and only."

Actually, that wasn't true. There were probably more, but this was the one that suited our client the best. According to Mr. Sampson, a weather witch who'd commissioned me to find a youth charm for him, it would keep the drinker looking ever young and beautiful. They'd still age—all the magic and the mages in the world hadn't figured out the secret of immortality—but they'd look good doing it. Mr. S planned to be the hottest weather witch on TV. Weather witches weren't usually meteorologists, but Mr. S liked being a semi-famous local celebrity.

Most of my jobs were on spec—Del found record of enchanted artifacts that possessed valuable magic, and I went to find them. But some jobs were on commission, and the chalice was one of them. No matter the job, we stayed away from artifacts from human archaeological sites. They had laws to protect their history—eventually someone would have noticed if I screwed with them. We try not to use magic around the humans, despite the Great Peace.

Besides, their artifacts had no magic, so they were worthless to us. We weren't in it for artifacts—we were in it for the magic. The problem was that magic could become unstable. After sitting around in an object for too long—anywhere from a few hundred years to a few

31

thousand, depending on the spell—it could cause some serious damage. Like fruit ripening on a tree, eventually it rots. Or in this case, explodes. Our operation was legal because we stuck to magical artifacts that were nearing the end of their life. Otherwise, we'd just be stealing. The Order of the Magica would have a problem with that—and we definitely didn't want to get on their bad side. And it felt crappy to steal something from an ancient culture that no longer existed.

I leaned on the counter and took a chocolate out of the candy bowl. Nix picked up the chalice and looked at it, squinting at the decorative etching that turned the golden goblet into a work of art.

"This one should be easy," she said as she set it down.

"You're going to do it now?" My stomach grumbled.

"Yeah. Only five minutes. It's a simple one. And the magic has gotten really unstable. Better to do it now. Then we're done for the night, and it's off my plate."

"Fine." But she was right. We tried not to leave the unstable magic sitting around in the shop. Last thing we needed was a spell going wild in here.

My stomach growled again, and I grabbed another chocolate, unwrapping it as Nix touched the goblet with her right hand, then hovered her palm over the counter. She closed her eyes, and the hum of magic took shape around her, complex and delicate.

Unlike me, Nix could use her magic, as long as she did it in small amounts. She practiced her magic more because it didn't result in explosions. She was so good at it that I could now barely sense her magic when she used it. The scent of flowers was so light you'd assume it was from a vase nearby.

Her hand glowed. Beneath it, a goblet slowly materialized. It glinted gold—an identical replica.

"Jeez, that was fast."

"Eh, it's gold."

Nix had a knack for replicating gold, even though what she created wasn't technically the same stuff. Just yellow metal. If we could have replicated gold, we probably wouldn't have been in the treasure hunting business in the first place.

"Now for the last step," she said as she hovered her left hand over the goblet.

Magic swirled up from the goblet and into her hand, like blue smoke. It shimmered, the smoke dancing beneath her palm. Once she'd gathered all the magic from the original chalice, she let it hover under her hand for a moment. She infused it with some of her own power, stabilizing it a bit. Once the shimmering faded, she transferred the now stabilized magic to her forged chalice by hovering her hand over it and forcing the blue smoke into the metal. Nix wasn't able to give the magic its original lifespan, but it'd last long enough that the buyer could use the magic they'd purchased. And it likely wouldn't blow up our shop.

"There. Ready for old Mr. Sampson. Hottest weather guy on TV for the last sixty years."

I grinned.

When we'd set up our shop, Nix had learned how to magically forge the artifacts I found so that we could put the originals back in their tombs or temples. It was part of our deal with the Magica—take just the magic. Only the oldest magic, since it was ready to expire anyway. Initially, we'd put the enchantments in regular old pieces of polished glass, but then we'd figured out we'd get more if we sold the magic encased in a replica. Sure, our buyers would like to own an original piece of ancient magical history to put on their mantel, but I wasn't willing to give them that. Not only was it illegal, I didn't like the idea of selling off pieces of history.

The memory of the shattered column sent a shiver through me. I hated when I caused damage like that. But worse, I hated the memory of that demon.

"Hey, you okay?" Nix asked.

I glanced up at her.

"You look a little rough," she said.

I glanced down at my dirty, black tank top and the honey-colored leather jacket that was now blackened with smoke. I got a whiff of my hair, which was even worse, and when I pulled a strand out of my ponytail, I saw that the red was almost completely gray from temple dust.

"Ugh." I dropped my hair.

"Not your hair, though you could use a shower." Nix brushed some dust off the shoulder of my jacket. "Looks ruined. Good thing you've got a hundred more of these. But I'm not talking about how you look. You just seem off."

I sighed. "Yeah. There was a demon in the temple."

"So? There's always a demon." She shrugged. "Almost always."

"Yeah." Demons were frequently called upon to guard tombs and temples because they made excellent henchmen if you were willing to spring them from their hell, but they really shouldn't be on earth. Getting rid of them was a big part of my job.

"You sent him back to hell, right? It's not like one got away."

I almost huffed a laugh but didn't have it in me. Nix knew how I liked to leave clean jobs behind. All demons sent back to hell. So far, my record was spotless. Though I wished I'd left that demon alive long enough to get more info out of him.

"Was it an extra awful demon?" Nix asked.

"No." Like mages and witches, demons had their own gifts. Some could get into your head and really screw around—make you see your worst nightmare, that kind of thing. "No. This one said something creepy. Really creepy."

Nix just raised her brows.

"He said I was one of the three. And"—I swallowed hard as my stomach turned—"FireSoul."

Nix's face turned serious, and her brown eyes darkened with fear. "What?"

I could almost feel her terror. I could certainly hear it.

"How could he know that? No one knows that," Nix said.

Just us.

It was hard to breathe. The memories always made it hard to breathe.

"We've been hiding for so long," I said. "It's been ten years since we woke in that field, and we've never told anyone what we are."

It was our most precious secret. The one that our lives depended upon.

"We have our concealment charms," Nix said. "They cost a fortune. We should be safe."

"Yeah, you're right." It'd taken us years to save up to buy the concealment charms and another year to find a supernatural to craft them. The spell should hide us from the eyes of any who sought to do us harm, with particular emphasis on my hazy memory of the man from my nightmares. If we ever ran into him, he would see us but not recognize us.

The charms were the only things that allowed us to settle in Magic's Bend. Without them, we'd have had to stay on the run.

Magic's Bend was the largest all-magic city in the US. It wasn't huge—no skyscrapers or anything—but we had a population of over sixty thousand. We'd moved here when we were twenty, right after buying our charms, thinking it'd be the best place to set up Ancient Magic. We'd been right.

I scrubbed a hand over my face, all the worry of the afternoon suddenly unbearably heavy on my shoulders. "I'm not going to worry about it for now. You're right, we have the concealment charms. I sent that demon back to his hell. He was an old demon—really strong. Maybe that's how he sensed what I am. But there's nothing we can do now. I just want to forget it."

Nix sighed and leaned against the counter. "No, you're right. We'll just have to wait and see if something weird happens."

I huffed a laugh. Weird. Like being thrown in the Prison for Magical Miscreants. "I'm going to grab a shower. I suddenly felt more grimy than hungry. Want to meet at Potions & Pastilles in twenty minutes?"

"Sure. I'm headed over now. Connor and Claire are both working tonight."

I grinned. It'd be good to see our friends. Our only friends, besides Del.

I waited while Nix put the forged chalice—complete with youth charm—in a box and set it on the shelf behind the counter for Mr. S. She put the original beneath the counter.

I'd return it to the tomb in a couple days. I'd also try to find someone to help me magically undo the damage to the ancient warrior goddess pillar. I hated to see a good woman laid low, not to mention the shitty feeling of having destroyed something so old. I didn't know my own history, so I didn't want to go around destroying someone else's.

We headed out of the shop. Nix shut the door behind her, then ran her hands around the edges of the door, triggering the enchantment that protected the shop. Only she, Del, or I could enter. Even breaking the windows wouldn't get you in if you weren't pre-approved by the enchantment.

Nix headed for the coffee shop/bar that sat left of us, and I went right. I lived in the converted factory above Ancient Magic—Nix and Del also had apartments there since we owned everything over the first floor—but the entrance was outside the shop.

It was a brisk summer evening in Magic's Bend, the sun only now starting to set even though it was nearly nine o'clock. Birds chirping across the street caught my attention. They hopped around on the top of a large, black SUV sitting in front of the park near my own car, Cecelia. My junker rarely had company. Normally people left their cars farther down the street for Potions & Pastilles. I ignored it as I unlocked the green door next to Ancient Magic. I pushed it open and climbed the narrow stairs leading to my apartment. My leg was killing me.

Though I'd been starving just moments ago, now all I wanted was a chance to wash off the dust and see if my leg needed a bandage. If I could wash away some of the crappy feelings from earlier today, all the better.

Ever since Del, Nix, and I had woken up in that field, all we'd wanted was to keep our secret and learn about our pasts. We still didn't know what had happened to us or our parents—and it drove me nuts—but we'd managed to keep our secret and build a great life for ourselves.

But the demon's words had threatened that. Big time. And it had left me shaken.

The stairs leading to our apartments were rickety and narrow. We'd meant to renovate them when we moved in, but had never gotten around to it. I passed the second floor, where Del lived. When I passed the third floor, where Nix lived, I stiffened.

Something felt…off.

I wasn't alone.

For magic's sake, I couldn't get a break.

Quietly, I drew my blades from the sheaths at my thighs and continued up the stairs. Halfway up, I could see the landing at my door. Long legs clad in jeans. A few steps higher and I could make out a broad chest covered in a dark gray t-shirt.

One more step and I laid eyes on the hottest, most dangerous looking guy I'd ever seen. Worse, the power that radiated off him was so intense my eyes almost crossed.

CHAPTER THREE

Not everyone could sense another's magic, but strong supernaturals could. The more powerful you were, the more completely you were hooked into the magic that was everywhere. You could sense other supernaturals—especially strong ones—easily. For me, the strongest magic hit all my senses instead of just one or two. This guy lit up all six, my dragon sense included.

His magic smelled like the forest, crisp and clean, but sounded like pounding ocean waves or roaring wind. It tasted of dark chocolate. I rubbed my tongue against the roof of my mouth as I took in the silver gray aura that surrounded him.

I couldn't pinpoint if he was a shifter or one of the Magica. Both? I shivered. Half-bloods were rare, but scary strong considering that they could draw from both being magic—the shifter side—and doing magic—the Magica side.

But it was the feel of his power that was really unusual. It felt good. Really good. Like a massage or a bubble bath or an amazing kiss. It freaked me out. The worst was my dragon sense, though. My dragon sense could only find things of value. And it tugged me toward this guy like he was a treasure chest full of gold.

He was valuable.

To me? That was nuts. But the pull was there, that familiar sense of being dragged toward something I wanted.

But I did not want him. The idea that part of me wanted something my brain didn't agree with was no good.

I'd only felt power that strong once, from the memory of the man we'd run from. And everything about his magic had been dark. It'd smelled and tasted like rot and felt like being stabbed with a thin knife. It wasn't like this guy's magic. But power that strong made me nervous. His magic alone was dangerous. If I used mine around him, he was strong enough to sense it. He might even figure out what I was.

"Care to explain what you're doing lurking outside my door?" I asked, keeping my knives at the ready.

How'd he get past the locked door downstairs?

"Waiting for you," he said. His voice had a hint of gravel to it, but in a pleasant way. A sexy way, but I didn't want to explore that until I was sure he wasn't here to kill me. Combined with the chiseled planes of his face and his athletic physique, he was the complete package.

He looked like a super model, but not quite the pretty kind. The kind that was a bit rough around the edges, with strong hands and chiseled features. He could model designer flannel as easily as suits. His dark hair and eyes would look amazing with either, but it was his lips that I had to drag my stupid gaze from.

He towered over my five-foot-seven-inch height. Six three, at least, I mused, sizing him up for a potential showdown. If it came down to it, I'd have to run. Between his magic and his strength, I wouldn't stand a chance.

"How'd you get in?" I asked, deciding to play nice and hoping this didn't go south. Perhaps he had a legit reason to be here, but the pessimist inside me said otherwise.

"You shouldn't leave your door unlocked."

"It wasn't."

"Then I got lucky."

"And by luck, you mean magic."

He shrugged one big shoulder and nodded.

"But you didn't use it to get into my place?" I asked. I tried to calm my racing heart, hoping his shifter senses couldn't pick it up. I didn't think he'd be able to find my troves even if he had gotten in—they were well hidden behind false walls—but I didn't like the possibility.

The corner of his mouth hiked up in a devastating smile. "That'd be just rude."

An exasperated puff of air escaped me. I shouldn't have been thinking about how hot or funny this guy was…but I couldn't help it. "Yeah, totally. This little bit of B&E"—I pointed to the stairs—"is totally cool."

He grinned again, looking too charming and sexy for my own good. This guy was killing me. "You're the expert, given your line of work."

"What do you know about me? And who are you?"

"I know you're Cassiopeia Clereaux, the best treasure hunter in Magic's Bend."

"Cass," I said. Only Del and Nix could call me Cassiopeia. I chose Cleraux, my last name, because it sounded good with Cass. It wasn't Irish, but I couldn't remember if I liked my life back there. "Why don't you tell me who you are?"

"Aidan Merrick."

"Oh hell," I breathed. I'd thought his power felt strange. "The Origin."

"That name's a bit much, don't you think?"

"Is it true? Can you shift into anything?" I didn't know much about shifter lore, but according to rumor, the Origin was the descendent of the original alpha. The first shifter—a griffon or a dragon, depending on who you talk to. There was one born every generation, and he or she had the power to shift into any animal at will.

"You'd have to get to know me better to find out. That's not really first date information."

My heart fluttered. "This isn't a date."

"It could be."

"I thought you were here about a job."

"I am. But then I saw you. I'd like to add on a date."

"No." I'd only ever heard of Aidan Merrick, never seen him in person. I knew he had a place in Magic's Bend, but the tabloids said he had a house on every continent. Now that I looked at him, he did seem a bit familiar. I only skimmed the tabloids when waiting at the grocery store. Now, I wished I had a few subscriptions. He was even more dangerous than I'd first thought.

"That's final, then?" he asked.

"Final?"

"About the date."

"Yeah."

He shrugged, a surprisingly elegant motion for such a big guy. "I'll ask again later. Maybe you'll change your mind if you get to know me."

"Uh…" I had no idea what to say. Hot, powerful millionaires didn't normally ask me out. That wasn't really my thing. "Why are you here again?"

"Two reasons. One, I want to know why you robbed a tomb on my property in Ireland. And two, I want to hire you."

No joke, my jaw almost dropped. I kept it closed through force of will alone. He owned the property that contained the tomb I'd just robbed? Had he seen the broken warrior goddess column? Double damn.

"Most landowners don't notice when I borrow something."

"I'm not most. And…borrow?"

No, he certainly wasn't most.

"I'm returning the chalice tomorrow," I said, moving up my timeline and hoping he wouldn't wonder about the enchantment that'd been removed from it. "And how did you know I'd taken it?"

"A guess."

Shit. So I'd given myself away. "How? That tomb was completely untouched when I found it. The entrance was hidden in a cliff face. No one has been there in millennia."

"I knew it was there, I just haven't entered it. It's an ancient holy place. I like to leave things as I find them. Unlike some people."

Guilt stabbed me over the warrior goddess.

"I'm fixing her tomorrow when I return the chalice"—I still had to find someone with the magic to actually help me do that—"but how'd you even know I was there? Or that it was me?"

"After I felt the magic that destroyed the warrior column, I went down there. Most of the enchantments were deactivated, but I knew only the best treasure hunter could get past them. That's you."

"Were they your enchantments? Was the demon your guard?" I knew he'd said he'd never been in there, but I couldn't keep myself from asking.

"Demon?"

The surprise on his face looked genuine.

My shoulders relaxed slightly. It felt like he was telling the truth, though I wasn't one hundred percent sure. It still scared the crap out of me that he might know what the demon had known. I was dead if he knew my secret, and so were Del and Nix.

"There was a demon guarding the tomb. I sent it back to its hell," I said.

"That's strange. I've never sensed a demon there before."

"Well he was there. It was common for the ancients to hire them to guard tombs, since they don't die like normal supernaturals do. And I'm returning the chalice, so no harm, no foul."

His head cocked to the side. "Is that how it works? Because I don't think so. If you do a job for me, however, we'll consider it even."

I chewed on my lip. "What kind of job?"

"Can we go in and talk about this?" He looked around the tiny landing, and I realized that I was still standing on the stairs below him.

"Uh, no," I blurted, then winced. I really didn't want him in my place. It wasn't fit for visitors. It was never fit for visitors.

"Then let's go for a drink somewhere and I'll explain."

Under normal circumstances, I might have considered it. But nothing about our encounter had been normal. And what he might know still freaked me out. I didn't think he knew what the demon had known—that was an old demon. Though Aidan was the Origin, he wasn't old, maybe late twenties.

"Just give me an idea of what the job is."

"I'm looking for the Scroll of Truth."

Recognition slammed into me and my heart raced, but I had no idea why. I'd never heard that name before, not that I remembered.

But then, my brain still started to melt when I tried to remember the first fifteen years of my life. Or at least, that was what it felt like. But that name sounded so familiar. I strained, trying to pull any details out of my mind that I could. Anything. Why did it sound so familiar?

Piercing pain shot through my head. I retreated.

"What is it?" I asked, trying to play it cool, act like I didn't really care.

"A compendium of knowledge about the strongest Magica and shifters."

Oh hell. I could see why he would want something like that. He was one of the most powerful magical beings out there. Powerful beings didn't like their secrets exposed, not if they could help it.

Problem was, I was also a powerful being, even if I didn't use that power.

I needed to think about this, but I couldn't focus around him. His power, and face, and body—the whole package—distracted me.

"Okay, I'll have a drink with you. So we can talk about this. But let me shower first." More than getting clean, I needed a second to myself. "There's a place a few doors down the street, a bar called The Flying Wizard. Why don't you meet me there?"

I'd have preferred to go to Potions & Pastilles where I could at least get something to eat, but I didn't want him around Nix, or my two friends who ran P & P, Connor and Claire.

He nodded. "Fair enough. I'll see you there."

His body almost brushed mine as he passed. I held my breath, swearing that the air between us actually sparked, then let myself into my apartment. I leaned against the door and let my head drop back against the wood.

Holy cow, it was a lot to absorb. I sucked in some calming breaths, but the sight of my boring little apartment did nothing to put me at ease.

I pushed off the door and crossed the living room to my bedroom, where I pressed my hand against an empty spot along the back wall. I bounced on my heels as I waited for the spell to ignite. It took only a second, but soon a door appeared. I pushed it open and entered my trove.

Calm immediately enveloped me. My heart slowed and my mind cleared as I looked around at the neat shelves full of weapons, boots, and leather jackets.

Treasure meant different things to different people. Right now, to me, it meant those three things. When I woke in that field with Nix and Del ten years ago, treasure was food and shelter. We followed our senses toward what we wanted most. It was how we survived, though it wasn't easy.

While a huge part of me didn't want to believe that I was a FireSoul, I had a hidden lair in my house that was filled with treasure. I lived on the whole top floor of an old factory, easily four thousand square feet. My apartment took up about a tenth of that. My trove took up the rest.

Like Smaug crouching on his piles of gold, I hoarded my valuables. Del and Nix had their own troves. We knew it was kinda weird and very dragon-like, but we couldn't help ourselves. I was perpetually broke because of my compulsion to fill this place up. I didn't like to steal anymore, not if I could help it.

Though I'd have loved to hang out there longer, I didn't have time to spend siphoning calm from this place. I grabbed a leather jacket off a hanger to replace the one I was wearing. I stank like a campfire. A quick glance at my boots showed they were in fine condition, so I returned to my bedroom and sealed the door behind me.

Though I felt a little better, a shower would really put me back on track.

I tossed the jacket on the bed and headed to the bathroom. My bathroom was as tiny and cramped as the stairwell. Every fixture was about sixty years old. Basically, it was a nightmare. I should have renovated it, but like I said—perpetually broke from feeding the beast.

On autopilot, I showered and dressed. My actual closet was pretty small since I preferred to stick to my uniform of jeans and tees. Carefully, I strapped my dagger sheaths to my thighs. They were hidden by an enchantment when I was around humans.

Why did Aidan want *my* help specifically? I was a good treasure hunter, the best in the city. Was it just because I'd successfully made it past the enchantments in his tomb? I didn't think he knew what the demon had said about me, but there was no guarantee.

His power set my internal alarms blaring. A huge part of me said that helping him was too dangerous. I needed to stay away from him, avoid allowing him to sense what I was. But the lure of the scroll was too much to resist. It could possess information about what I was. About why I'd awoken in a field at fifteen with no memories.

I really wanted those memories back. And even if it couldn't help me get my memories back, I owed him. I'd broken in to the ancient temple on his land.

So, my decision to help him had nothing do to with the fact that I couldn't stop thinking about his lips. No way.

"Idiot," I muttered as I tugged my jacket on. This one was a slightly darker brown leather than my other, closely fitted to look good but loose enough that I could fight in it. I might have worn any old tees and jeans, but my boots and my jackets were important. I'd been eyeing this one online for months before I had the money for it. I just hoped it lasted longer than the other.

I locked up behind me and headed down the stairs, trying not to think of how it had felt when Aidan had almost brushed up against me. I had real problems to worry about, and that wasn't going to be one of them.

Night had fallen by the time I got outside. The evening birds had been replaced with crickets, and the lamps in the park across the street now threw their yellow glow over the asphalt. Ancient Magic was quiet and dark as I passed it, and my stomach grumbled as I glanced longingly into Potions & Pastilles, which was next door.

My friends Connor and Claire—siblings—ran Potions & Pastilles. I spent a lot of my time there when I wasn't on a job, drinking coffee and shopping on the internet for my three weaknesses. During the day, P & P was a coffee house with a wide variety of sweets. At night, it turned into a bar that served a small selection of beers and a large selection of whiskey. Very hipster Oregon, but I liked it. There was always food, and it was always good.

Inside, dangling mason jar lights glinted warmly off the small, round, wooden tables, and original—though of questionable quality—artwork hung on the wall. Connor was behind the small bar, and I assumed Claire was in the kitchen. Nix sat talking to a man, a smile stretched across her face.

She hadn't mentioned that she had a date. He was pretty hot from the back—tall, broad shouldered, dark haired. Go Nix. When he turned to look at the wall, I caught sight of his profile.

Aidan.

Annoyance seethed through me. I'd told him to meet me at The Flying Wizard for this exact freaking reason. And I couldn't even storm in there and yell at him, because that might make him suspicious.

Inside, Nix laughed at something Aidan said. Connor laughed too, a goofy smile on his face. My friends liked him. The five of us—Nix, Del, Connor, Claire, and I—were all pretty close. My friends weren't dumb. If they were giving him the stamp of approval, I had to take that into account.

I sighed and pushed into P & P. The smell of buttery pastry and savory meat from the oven enveloped me, and my stomach grumbled. The kitchen at P & P was small— it was really more of a bar and coffee house than a restaurant. Claire and Connor were from Cornwall, home of the Cornish Pasty, a good thing to sell out of a small space. I was pretty much addicted to them.

"Hey," I said when I reached their table, trying to stifle the sound of annoyance in my voice. "This isn't The Flying Wizard."

Aidan turned his too-handsome face toward me. I repressed a scowl at the desire that streaked through me.

"They didn't have food," he said. "I thought you'd be hungry after your raid."

Nix shot me a how-the-heck-do-you-know-this-guy look.

Later, I tried to say without words.

"I ordered you two steak and stiltons," he said.

At his words, Claire came out of the back with a plate carrying two golden brown pasties. My stomach grumbled as the divine scent wrapped around me. I tried to ignore how cool it was that he'd thought of feeding me. If there was one thing I was into, it was guys getting me food. Anyone getting me food, really.

"Thanks." I dragged a chair over to their table and sat down between him and Nix. The table was small enough that our knees almost touched. I scooted away and looked at Claire instead of him.

Her brown hair fell in waves around her face, and she was dressed for the kitchen in an apron that covered her t-shirt and jeans, though I hadn't seen her in here the last couple of days. "How'd your last job go?"

"Good. Caught the bloke as he was leaving the bank."

"That's convenient." Claire was a Fire Mage with a dash of Hearth Witch, hence the coffee shop. By day, she was a mercenary. Magical organizations hired her to handle problems. She kicked ass but had an unquenchable desire to make excellent coffee and pastries. Connor hadn't inherited any of his mother's Fire Mage powers and was all Hearth Witch, so he ran their shop most of the time. He was wickedly good at potions, which lent itself to preparing the enchanted coffees they offered.

"Yeah, it was an easy job. You want the usual?" Claire asked, her dark eyes alight with the same who-is-this-dude look that the others had sent my way.

Everyone thought it was weird as hell that I was hanging out with one of the wealthiest, most powerful guys in the world. I agreed.

"Uh, no thanks. A latte?" PBR was my drink of choice in the evenings, even though everyone made fun of me for drinking the beer of hipsters and hillbillies. I didn't drink a lot, but I was picky about it when I did. But if I was going to be chatting with Aidan about the scroll—or anything really—I needed to be on my game.

"Sure thing," Claire said.

"How'd it go today?" Connor asked from behind the counter as he crafted my latte. He had the same dark hair as Claire and also favored her P & P uniform of jeans and a t-shirt topped with an apron.

"Ah, good," I said, glancing awkwardly at Aidan. Connor liked to hear about the enchantments and demons in each tomb or temple that I raided, but now wasn't the time for a play-by-play. "I'll tell you about it later."

"Cool." He brought my coffee over.

"Thanks." I dug into the pasties.

"I'm headed out," Nix said. "Good to meet you, Aidan."

"See you later," I said, grateful she was getting away from Aidan. She and the others might have approved of him, but he was still too much of an unknown for me to be comfortable trusting him around the people I loved.

I turned to Aidan and really looked at him for the first time since entering P & P. I'd never seen a guy make a gray t-shirt look so good. It was a dark gray, the same color as his eyes. I'd thought they were brown.

"Have you eaten?" I asked, trying to distract myself from his eyes. He had a pint of some kind of dark beer in front of him.

"Yes. The pasties were excellent."

"So, tell me more about this scroll," I said between bites. "But quietly, I don't want to drag Connor or Claire into this."

"What do you want to know?"

"What else is written in it? I've never heard of it before, but it sounds pretty valuable."

"It is. It contains information about all the most powerful species of supernaturals. Strengths and weaknesses. I don't have many weaknesses, but I don't want anyone knowing them."

"Don't blame you." I popped the last bite of pasty into my mouth.

"And according to a reference I just found in an old text, it's a prophetic scroll. It contains a list of the names and descriptions of individuals who belong to all the most powerful species. Past and present."

I choked on my pasty. Names and descriptions? Past and present?

That meant me.

CHAPTER FOUR

Aidan passed me a glass of water as I coughed, trying to clear the pasty from my throat.

Okay, this had suddenly gotten a hell of a lot worse. My mind raced like a hamster in a wheel. The scroll might not actually exist. Or it might not have the information he said it had.

But if it did, it would include my name under the heading FireSoul, subheading To Be Killed On Sight. Or, alternate, To Be Imprisoned For Life.

Oh, this was bad.

"Are you all right?" Aidan asked, concern in his dark eyes.

"Fine, totally fine. Just swallowed wrong." I nodded, trying to look normal and knowing I'd failed. Was there any way I could do this job without him? Steal it and destroy it before he saw it?

Unless he told me some really key details about the scroll, no. I didn't have enough to go on. For my tracking ability to work, I needed a couple things. First, somebody needed to really want whatever I was looking for. My dragon sense was based on covetousness. That was no problem. I wanted that scroll. Bad.

But I also needed to know at least one or two intimate details about the object or person I sought. More was better. Images were the best, but knowledge of who made it or something like that would help. Just enough for my magic to latch on and take me there.

He'd have to give me that information. Then I'd get it and have Nix make a copy that omitted our information.

"So, this scroll sounds pretty interesting," I said. "I'll take the job. Half price because I broke into your tomb." I'd do it for free, but I didn't want him thinking I was too eager.

"Excellent. We'll leave tomorrow."

What the heck? That wasn't part of my plan. "We? I work alone."

"I'll help you. It could be dangerous."

"Dangerous is my day job," I said. I winced, realizing I sounded like a jacked-up meathead from an action movie. But for magic's sake, I walked around with daggers strapped to my thighs. You'd think it'd be obvious that I could handle myself. "I'll take care of it. You don't need to worry."

"I know you can take care of yourself," he said, his dark eyes serious. "But I want this scroll. Badly. And I don't trust anyone else with it. I'll come along."

Damn. I waffled, but he looked determined. "All right. Tomorrow. Can you tell me a little more about the scroll?" Maybe if he told me enough, I could find it tonight.

He nodded and leaned back in his chair, long and lean muscles stretching out. I sagged a bit, grateful he didn't suspect me.

"The scroll was written over a thousand years ago by monks who lived on an island off the coast of Ireland," he said.

Nerves prickled along my skin. That was the third time today that Ireland had come up. First I raided a tomb there, then Aidan, who owned an estate there, showed up, and now these monks. I didn't like it. I worked all over the world. Today was my first job in Ireland in years. And it had come complete with a demon who knew I was a FireSoul and a handsome, dangerous stranger who wanted me to find a scroll that could spell my death.

Yeah, it was weird.

"The monks are still the only ones who live on the island," Aidan said. "They're supernaturals, but they choose to rely on study and contemplation rather than magic. They're called the Holy Order of Knowledge. Their entire purpose is to record every bit of knowledge about the supernatural world that they can. The Scroll of Truth was created by their greatest seer before his death. He used his power to write about the future, which is why my name is probably in it even though it was written long before my birth. But it was stolen."

"By whom?"

"I don't know."

"If it's been missing for so long, how do you even know about it?"

"I keep a seer on retainer. She scries for threats to me and my enterprises every year. This year, she sensed a threat in the form of the scroll. She thinks someone else is trying to find it. But all she could see was the name of the scroll and that the Order of Holy Knowledge created it. I want to find it before the other person does."

Oh hell. This had just gotten worse. Someone else was after it? Seers couldn't see every aspect of the future, but they were infallible about what they could see. "Do you know anything about who is hunting it?"

"No. Just that someone is."

"Know anything else about it?"

"That's it."

"It might be enough." I'd gone on way less in the past. I had its name—the Scroll of Truth—who'd made it and what it was made of. I'd found the Chalice of Youth with just a name and the knowledge that it was made of gold. But then, it was really, really easy for me to find gold.

I closed my eyes and tried to envision the scroll. I focused on the names—Scroll of Truth and the Order of Holy Knowledge. My mind reached out, seeking the thread that would tie about my middle, but pain slammed into me.

I gasped and slumped forward in my chair, my head pounding. I reached up and cupped my forehead. This had never happened before. Why did this scroll make me feel this way? First in the stairwell and now here.

Was it because it contained information about my past? It made me even more determined to find it. No question, it involved me. Any time I tried to think about something important from my past, the pain came.

"Are you all right?" Aidan asked.

"Fine, it's just been a really long day. Trying to find things with my mind is really draining," I lied. "Can we visit the monks? I need a bit more information."

"Yes. We'll take my plane."

His plane? He had a freaking plane? I didn't want to get on his plane. I wanted to use a transportation charm and get there now, but I'd used my last one in the temple earlier today.

If the monks lived in Ireland, his plane was my best bet. I could catch a commercial flight, but then I'd have to ask where exactly they lived, and by the time I got there, he would most likely be there already.

It looked like I wouldn't be sneaking off on my own after all. We'd do this together, and I'd figure out the rest later. And I didn't hate the idea of hanging out with him, even though I knew it was a bad idea.

"All right. When can we leave?" I asked.

"Tonight. There's a bed on the plane."

"A bed?" He had a plane with bedrooms? I quirked a brow at him, suspicious. "For?"

He grinned. "Sleeping. Just sleeping. You've got to be beat after destroying the temple in Murreagh."

"Good. Don't get any ideas."

He put up his hands. "Wouldn't dream of it. I want that date first."

The look he gave me was pretty obvious. He liked what he saw. I blushed. I really wouldn't say no to a cup of coffee with him under different circumstances, even though it was a really dumb idea. If I hung out with him too long and got into a situation where I had to use my power, he was strong enough to suspect what I was.

I stood. "Business only, pal. But let's get started. Ireland's far away."

Aidan paid our bill, which I had no problem with. I was on the clock now. It wasn't a date. He met me by the door, dwarfing me with his size.

"I'm going to grab a bag, okay? Wait here."

He looked like he wanted to offer to come up to my place, but no way was that happening. I ran out before he could say anything.

The scent of rain was on the air as I raced down the sidewalk and let myself into my building. Nix burst out of her apartment door as I ran by.

"What's the deal with Aidan Merrick?" She followed me up the steps. "You suddenly start dating one of the richest, most powerful hybrids in the world and don't tell me?"

"We're not dating," I said as I let myself into my apartment. She slipped in behind me, and I locked the door. "He showed up with a job about a scroll."

"Scroll? What's inside it?"

"It could tell people what we are."

Nix stepped back, her eyes wide. "Are you serious?"

"Yeah. And Aidan said someone else is after it, too."

"That's weird. Right after you ran into a demon who knew we were FireSouls? Too much coincidence."

"I know. That's why I'm going to go get that scroll and destroy it. I might need you to make a forged version if there's time. Without the information about us."

"Yeah, no kidding. But this is nuts." She shook her head. "I talked to Connor and Claire. They both think he's cool. And I really liked him."

A bit of the tension faded out of me at the news that Connor and Claire trusted Aidan. Connor was a better judge, as he was all Hearth Witch, but Claire's opinion was good too, considering she had a bit of Hearth Witch in her. Hearth witches were really good at reading people's intentions. Something about protecting hearth and home. And because Aidan had been in their shop and they lived in the back, their powers had been amplified when they'd assessed him.

I couldn't trust him one hundred percent, but he had the stamp of approval from Connor and Claire. He was probably safe.

Until he learned what I was.

Something I wasn't going to let happen.

Nix peppered me with questions as I threw a couple changes of clothes into a small duffle. I had no idea how long we'd be gone, but I hoped not more than a couple days.

"Right, I'm out of here," I said when I was done.

We left my apartment and headed down the stairs.

"You've got your charm if you need me," Nix said at her door.

"Yeah, thanks." I hugged her and turned to go, but a thought popped into my head. I spun around. "Hey, will you go ask Dr. Garriso about the scroll and call me if you learn anything?"

Dr. Garriso was our contact at the local museum and a scholar of all things magical history. We usually consulted him with questions about the artifacts we found. I loved his book-filled office but didn't have time to go see him now, and he really preferred to speak in person.

"Yeah. Good idea!"

"Thanks." I turned and took the stairs two at a time, hurrying to meet Aidan. As excited as I was to see him—which was so dumb, I knew it was—I still patted the dagger on my right leg. Old habits and all.

Aidan stood across the street, leaning against the big SUV I'd noticed earlier. Most of his body was in shadow, but it was hard not to notice his height or the breadth of his shoulders. How was it fair that one of the strongest supernaturals in the world was also built like a world-class athlete and looked like a model?

I scowled. It was unnatural, and dangerous for my sanity.

"Ready?" he asked.

"Yep, let's get a move on." I climbed into his car. It was nondescript, but way nicer than my junker. Cars were not one of the things I considered to be treasure. Thus, Cecilia was an old broad on her last legs. "Is your plane at the Fairfield Airport?"

"Yes," he said as he pulled out onto the street. "I've told them to expect us."

His phone rang. He picked it up. "Merrick."

I perked up when he spoke. Eavesdropping wasn't cool, but it counted as extenuating circumstances when mysterious, powerful strangers showed up on your door and needed your help with something that threatened your life.

But his words were in another language. Not Irish or English, so I was out of luck. I gave up listening as we drove through the quiet streets of Magic's Bend. It had started raining, and the streets were empty.

By the time Aidan hung up the phone, we were pulling up to the small airport at the edge of town. Magic's Bend sat on the Pacific, with a deep water port that wasn't used very often. There wasn't much in the way of suburbs, except on the south side of town where the rich people lived, so the rest of the city backed up to the forest and mountains. The airport was positioned right at the edge of town.

Aidan drove completely around the main terminal to the back. Sitting apart from the small fleet of commercial jets was a sleek private plane, far bigger than I'd expected.

Aidan stopped the car beside the stairs that lead up to the plane. I hopped out.

"I'll take that for you." A bright-eyed flight attendant—a guy only a couple years younger than me—held out his hand for my bag.

"Ah, I'm fine." I smiled, then headed up the stairs.

I whistled when I stepped into the plane. His car might have been nondescript, but his plane was anything but. Creamy leather and sleek wood decorated the space. The seats looked huge and comfortable, and there was even a couch in the back. I stepped in and turned to him. I was about to ask him how he afforded such a ridiculous plane when a thought occurred to me.

"How come your plane is here if you were in Ireland earlier today? You didn't have time to fly here."

"Magic's Bend is my home base," he said as he stepped into the plane. "I was just at my place in Ireland for the week. I took a portal charm to get here."

"But wouldn't that leave your plane back in Ireland?"

"I flew commercial," he said as he walked to the small kitchen in the front. A curtain was pulled back, but when closed, it would conceal the small space. He grabbed two bottles of water from the fridge and handed me one. "If it's just me, I feel like a jerk taking this thing. It burns a lot of fuel to carry just one person."

"So you're an environmentalist?"

"Not a good one." He held up the plastic bottle in his hand and nodded to it. "But I try to do okay about the obvious stuff. Taking this jet for just me is one of those things."

"But you'll take it tonight."

He shrugged. "You need to sleep, and this one has a bed."

Huh. That was…nice of him. I'd never had a guy be thoughtful enough to offer me a plane before. Then again, I'd never known a guy with a plane before. Who did?

"Thanks," I said.

The captain came out of the cockpit. "If you'll take your seats, we're about to take off."

"Thanks, Tom," Aidan said.

I found a seat in the middle and sank into it. I stifled a moan. It was so dang comfortable. After fighting the demon and then immediately dealing with Aidan, I'd been too distracted to realize how much my whole body hurt. Especially my leg.

"You all right?" Aidan asked as he took the seat next to me. The plane rumbled as it taxied down the runway. He was close enough to me that I could smell the fresh forest scent of him. Most shifters had a slightly musky scent. Not bad, just animalistic. But he didn't. Because he was the Origin, maybe.

"I'm fine," I said. "Just bruised up my leg pretty bad in the temple. I heal quickly, though."

"I've got some healing ability if you want me to give it some help."

I glanced up into his dark gaze. My breath caught. Healing meant touching. Not a lot, but any kind of touching with a guy like Aidan…

"Uhhh…." Wow, I was great with words.

CHAPTER FIVE

"It's no problem," he said. "It'll only take a moment."

It was a bad idea, but I couldn't help myself. The plane was now ascending into the sky, and it felt like I was leaving the real world behind. "Okay. It's my leg. Left shin."

I held my breath as he laid his big palm against my leg. Even through my tall boots, I could feel the heat of him. Worse, I could feel his magic. I thought just standing near him was sensory overload? Though his hand stayed still, his magic caressed me, starting at my leg and working its way up. It felt amazing—comforting and tingly at the same time. About the best thing I'd ever felt.

I closed my eyes and tried to control my breathing. I did not want him to know how much I liked this. If he moved his hand up my leg, I wasn't entirely certain I would stop him. Normally I was great at shutting down guys who got handsy. But Aidan was different.

I liked him. I even liked that he was a little bit dangerous. Which definitely meant I needed to set up an appointment with a shrink. But for now, trapped in this plane, I just wanted to focus on how good this felt.

Too soon, he removed his hand. Disappointment surged through me. But as my mind cleared, relief came. Touching Aidan had been a bad idea. Something so little had clouded my mind. That was way too risky. I needed to stay sharp. Keep my guard up. I tried to shake the memory of his touch away and moved my leg.

Good as new.

"Thanks," I said.

That was my cue. I liked him. Too much, and I had to get out of here.

"I'm going to hit the hay." I stood and eyed the couch at the back of the plane. It looked divine. Squishy and soft. "Is there a blanket for that couch?"

"Take the bed," he said. "The door in the back leads to a bedroom."

"Is there only one bedroom?"

"Yes, but I'll take the couch."

I eyed his tall frame. "You're not exactly going to fit on it."

"I'll manage. Take the bed."

I was so tired, and I really wanted some space to myself. A door between me and Aidan would help me get my head on straight.

"Okay, thanks." I grabbed my bag and headed to the back.

The gleaming wooden door opened to reveal a luxurious bedroom suite. It was modern and sleek, but the bed looked like heaven. I passed out in seconds; the last thought in my head was of Aidan's hand on my leg.

I got lucky. If I dreamed of Aidan, I didn't remember it by the time I woke. The jolt of the plane touching down on the runway jerked me from sleep. I scrambled out of bed and threw on fresh clothes. Just a change of underwear and shirt. My jeans were fine. I usually wore them till they were destroyed anyway. Laundry was lame.

When I entered the main cabin, the exterior door was open, and a fresh breeze blew inside.

"Morning, sleepyhead," Aidan said. He stood in the small kitchenette, looking refreshed and way too handsome after sleeping on that tiny couch all night. "I made some coffee to go. Want some?"

"Sure."

"A lot of cream, right?"

"How'd you know?" I didn't like him knowing things about me. Even innocuous things like this.

"You ordered a latte last night, so you like wimpy coffee."

And he was observant. Dangerous. "Wimpy coffee? I suppose you drink yours black?"

"Black as my heart."

I laughed. I didn't trust him. But I liked him. "You got a muffin to go with that?"

"Blueberry or bran? There's a basket here with both."

"Bran. It sounds healthy, but tastes delicious."

He pulled one out of the basket and handed it to me along with my coffee.

"Ready?" he asked. "There's a car waiting. We can head to the coast now. I've got a boat on stand-by."

"Is there a type of transportation you can't access immediately?" This guy had everything.

"No."

"Spaceship?"

"My company, Origin Enterprises, is in the final testing phase of a shuttle that's meant to carry valuables to a safe deposit bank on the moon. If you can wait a year or so—until we're sure it won't blow up—I can even get you a seat on that."

"The moon?" I'd really thought I'd stump him with the spaceship thing.

"Safest place for valuables. Even you can't break in there."

I frowned. "Huh. That would really kill my business model."

"No doubt." He nodded to the stairs. " Ready?"

"Yeah." I made my way down the stairs to a white Range Rover. The rolling green of the Irish countryside spread out before me. The scent of grass and the lingering bite of jet fuel mingled in the cool air. I climbed down the rickety stairs, hoping I wouldn't fall on my face. These little landing stairs were always the worst.

On the ground, a red-haired man greeted us. He was in his forties with freckles and a friendly smile.

"Welcome back, sir." He handed Aidan a set of keys.

"Thank you, Patrick," Aidan said.

"Not a problem. I hope you have a fine visit."

"Give my best to your wife."

"She'll be delighted to hear it!" Patrick nodded goodbye and walked toward the terminal.

"Where are we?" I asked. I'd only ever been through the Dublin airport.

"Secret location." Aidan held the passenger side door open for me, and I climbed in, balancing my coffee and my bag.

"Seriously though, where are we?" I asked before I sipped my coffee. Not bad.

"Private air strip in the southwest. We're headed to the coast now."

It took us about an hour to get to the little port. I was silent most of the drive. Though Ireland was beautiful, being here put me on edge, like I was walking along the Cliffs of Moher in a strong easterly wind.

If I was Irish—I hated that I couldn't say for certain because I didn't remember—this might be the place that we'd fled. The person we ran from might still live here.

When Nix, Del, and I had awoken in the field, we'd quickly figured out that we were in America. But Irish had been far easier for us to speak. We still didn't know why, but maybe we'd run from here.

I was relieved when we finally arrived in the little port. I wanted to get off land. A grizzled old man with white hair and a fisherman's cap waited for us on the single dock. A pipe puffed at his mouth.

"Aidan, my lad, good to see you," he said. "Visiting the monks?"

"Yes," Aidan said. "Thanks for lending us your boat."

"Well you're paying me a pretty penny now, so it's no hardship." The man handed over a key and nodded to the rickety fishing boat that bobbed at the dock. It was red, though the paint peeled, and was a distinctly charming sight in its sunny setting.

"Thank you, Mack," Aidan said. "I'll bring her back in one piece."

I climbed aboard and we set off.

"Not the quickest boat," I said as we bounced over the waves. "But it has charm."

"The faster boats are in the bigger tourist towns. Better to stay under the radar."

That, I could agree with. Though this was just recon, it was good practice to avoid humans when doing something that could go magically south.

"Is that it?" I asked, shielding my eyes against the sun as I looked over the glittering waves to a steep, craggy mountain that jutted out of the sea. I'd never seen a place so desolate. How could anyone live on the shear rock cliffs?

"It is. Monks have been living there for two thousand years."

"Jeeze. Peaceful, I guess. But being locked up there for my whole life—no thanks."

The jagged cliffs soared above us as we pulled the boat up to a small floating dock.

The sound of screams and blasts of magic rent the air.

"What the hell?" I glanced at Aidan.

"So much for peaceful." He grabbed a line and leapt off the boat onto the dock.

I hopped out as he tied off the boat, charging up the stone steps without waiting for him. They were nearly vertical, but the sound of a fight pushed me forward.

On the cliffs above, I spied a collection of strange beehive-shaped stone structures. It'd be quicker to climb over the rock ledge to my right rather than take the stairs that curved around.

Aidan's footsteps sounded and I turned.

"Give me a boost," I said.

He eyed the seven-foot tall cliff that I needed to get over and nodded, then grabbed me around the waist and practically threw me over. I scrambled up as he pulled himself gracefully onto the rock to my left.

Wind whipped as I turned to face the buildings. They rose behind the jutting rock and scraggly grass ahead. Shouts sounded from the largest one, a long building made entirely of stone. The walls curved inward at the top to form a curved roof. Aidan and I charged it, stooping low under the small door.

The dimness blinded me for a moment. Candles illuminated the space, shining light on the combatants. There were at least a dozen monks, all clad in drab brown robes, fighting five dudes who looked like special ops goons from an action flick. Though *fighting* was a bit of an exaggeration. Despite their numbers, the monks were heavily outmanned. Most threw ineffectual punches while others launched weak blasts of power.

"Demons," I said when I spotted their dark gray skin. Good. I hated fighting other supernaturals because I was scared I might kill them and take their power.

Demons didn't really die, so they couldn't transfer power.

These looked a lot like the one that had called me a FireSoul, but most species of demons had gray skin. There wasn't a sun in most of the hells. I'd wait to see if they threw smoke before I got nervous.

I glanced at Aidan. "Leave one alive?"

"Yes. I want to know why the hell they're here."

I pulled my daggers from their sheaths and charged into the fray, toward a tall demon grappling with a monk. I wanted to throw Righty, but they were moving too quickly. Nailing a man of God with my dagger sounded like a bad idea.

I jumped onto a bench and launched myself off of it, crashing down on top of them. I shoved the monk out of the way with my foot and plunged Righty into the demon's left shoulder. He roared, his ugly face twisting in pain.

Agony seared my side and stole my breath. Warm blood soaked into my clothes. I assumed he'd swiped me with a knife but didn't look. His fist crashed down on my back, a punishing blow that sent pain radiating through my body.

That was why I liked to throw my knives.

I grabbed one of the demon's horns, pressing his head back onto the stone floor and stabbing him in the throat with my other knife.

Warm blood sprayed my face and I gagged.

Ugh. The worst. I scrambled off the demon. A second later, he strangled in his last breath. He'd disappear soon, his body returning to its hell. With my sleeve, I scrubbed some of the blood from around my eyes, then bent down to snag Righty, which protruded from his shoulder. Pain sang through me from the demon's blows. I glanced at my side and saw a long gash along my ribs. My back ached. Felt like a few broken ribs, damn it.

At least he hadn't gotten his blade between them. I was going to live, so I considered it a win.

A demon shrieked and I spun, startled by the sound of fear. Demons were never afraid. They were single-minded, inhuman in their desire to accomplish their goals. Fear didn't usually affect them. It was one of the main reasons they were used as minions to guard treasure or to carry out evil deeds.

"Holy hell," I breathed.

An enormous griffon stood at the side of the room, twice as big as a lion. It was beautiful, if you didn't mind being terrified. Enormous wings stretched out from its powerful back, arching up over a massive, leonine body. Its head was almost birdlike, but that was no delicate beak. It could pick up cows with that thing.

Where the hell had it come from? I glanced around.

Aidan was gone.

Oh, hell no.

But of course. That was Aidan. My sidekick was a freaking griffon. Though if he was a griffon, I was probably the sidekick in this situation.

Beast-Aidan launched himself off the floor and leapt upon two demons, grabbing each in a powerful front claw and smashing them against the ground.

Since it seemed Aidan had that side of the room well taken care of, I spun and eyed the other side. A demon was shaking a monk by his robe, demanding, "Where is it?"

The monk babbled in Irish, seeming unable to understand English.

Rage seethed in my chest. I didn't like bullies. This was the demon I'd save for questioning. I couldn't be sure the griffon would keep any alive.

I pushed aside the pain that throbbed at my back and side and charged the demon, flinging Righty as I ran. It sank into his arm. The demon grunted and looked up at me, then glanced around at the carnage Aidan and I had wrought. Only one of its brethren remained.

Nope, none. Aidan had ripped its head off with his beak. The head bounced across the stone before finally disappearing. I swallowed bile and looked at the remaining demon.

His eyes widened. I lunged at him, tackling him to the ground. He was enormous and sweaty beneath me.

When I opened my mouth to demand why he was there, something huge and golden flew in front of my face and slammed into the demon's head. I surged backwards as blood sprayed. Panting, I looked up at the monk who'd slammed an enormous ornamental candlestick onto the demon's skull.

The monk grinned proudly at me and said in Irish, "I saved you, lass. Sent that demon straight back to hell!"

Damn it. That was the last one we could have questioned.

"Uh, thank you," I said in Irish. I didn't want to piss off the monk who could give me answers about the scroll. And he was so proud of himself that I didn't have the heart.

Strong arms pulled me up. Shock sent my heart slamming into my ribs. Was there another demon still alive? I lashed out with Righty. Aidan caught my arm, the blade an inch from his face. I stepped back, breathing hard. He was human again, dressed in the same clothes.

"Are they all dead?" I sheathed Righty and Lefty. The adrenaline of the fight faded, and pain seared through me again. I pressed my arm to the wound in my side, wincing.

"Yes." Aidan glanced at my arm. "Are you all right?"

"I'm okay." At least, I thought I was. "Mostly I'm pissed we didn't keep one alive. I want to know why they were here."

"Me too. Though if I had to guess, it might have been for the scroll." He touched my arm, the one that was covering my wound. "Let me see that."

"Later," I said as I turned back to the monk who'd crushed the last demon's skull.

Three other monks approached us. All were breathing heavily, fear in their eyes.

Around us, the rest climbed to their feet. The interior of their cathedral was a mess. Turned over tables and shattered chairs littered the ground. At least none of the torches had started a fire.

"Thank you," the tallest monk said in Irish. "We were overwhelmed. Our warrior brother is away on a pilgrimage. We were not prepared for an attack.

Normally, he would protect us. Though we are supernaturals, we do not practice our skills."

"It was our pleasure," Aidan said, his voice smooth.

Our pleasure? It was hard to reconcile that this was the same guy who'd torn off a demon's head with his beak. Either way, I'd want him at my back in any fight.

"Do you know why the demons were here?" I asked in Irish.

"No. We only speak Irish, but they did not speak our tongue. They seemed to be demanding something, but I do not know what."

So they hadn't gotten the information they'd come for because they couldn't speak Irish. Good. "Do you often have attacks like this?"

The monk nodded. "Thieves and raiders come every few years. Sometimes as infrequently as a decade. It was worse with the Vikings, but even modern brigands would like to steal our holy relics."

He gestured to several large chests that sat at one side of the room. My dragon sense tugged at me as I looked at them. Logic said that they were full of golden goodies. My sense for treasure confirmed it.

Oh, how I'd love to poke around in those chests. Though my personal brand of treasure ran along the lines of quality leather goods and sharp, pointy things, I couldn't help but get a tingly sense of desire whenever I saw gold. I'd always feared that if I took some, I'd really turn into a FireSoul, crouched on my horde of gold like Scrooge McDuck.

"You think they were here for the gold?" I asked, though I doubted it.

The monk nodded. "It's what most thieves want."

True enough.

"But why are you here?" the monk asked.

"We're looking for the Scroll of Truth," Aidan said.

"Ah, yes. An interesting document." The monk folded his hands in front of him, the long brown sleeves of his robe draping to the floor. "That was stolen long ago. But we do not know where it is."

"Could you provide us with any information about it?" Aidan asked. "We'll return it if we find it."

I wondered if he was telling the truth.

The monk stared hard at Aidan. Perhaps he believed him, because he began to describe the scroll. The wood of the rollers, the colors of the inks used, what was written inside.

I listened with half an ear, but I no longer needed that type of detail. Now that I wasn't distracted by the demons, I could focus on my surroundings. I tried to push the pain to the back of my mind.

This was where the scroll had been written. A thousand years ago, somewhere in this dark space, a monk had sat crouched over one of the little tables, painstakingly scratching out words on vellum. It had taken years; I could almost see it in my mind. Just being in the place where so much effort had been poured into the scroll set my dragon sense alight.

I laid a hand on Aidan's arm, trying not to think about how big and hard it was, and gave him a look. I hoped it said, *We're good here.*

He seemed to get it. When the monk trailed off, he said, "Thank you. That was very helpful. We'll let you know if we find it."

The monk nodded. We said our goodbyes and left. I tried to keep my gaze off the chests full of gold as I limped out, but I didn't succeed. I needed a twelve-step program or something.

We took the stone steps that wound down the mountain. It didn't take us long to make our way back to the little dock.

"I want to look at that wound now," Aidan said as we climbed onto the boat.

It hurt badly enough that I removed my arm to show him.

"That looks rough," he said. "Why did you fight hand to hand? You should have used your magic."

"Those demons didn't have much to reflect back. And I'm a fairly weak mage." The first part was true. "Can you do something about this?" I asked to distract him, pointing at my wound.

He glanced at me like he wanted to ask more questions, but I tried to look like I was in pain. I even threw in a little whimper.

"Move your arm to the side," he said, but it still seemed like he was thinking about why I hadn't used my powers. Maybe it was paranoia on my part, but paranoia had kept me alive for a long time. We were good buddies.

I moved my arm away from the wound to give him room. I tried to focus on the bobbing of the boat beneath us as he laid his big palm gently against the gash.

I winced, then sighed in relief as warmth radiated through me. Slowly, the flesh knitted back together.

It was still sore when he removed his hand, but it felt a heck of a lot better.

"Anywhere else?" he asked.

I shifted, wincing as more pain radiated from my back. It felt a bit better than it had at first. "Just my back, but I don't think anything is broken."

"Let me see. Turn."

I turned, pinning my gaze on the open sea. Now that I no longer had a gaping wound in my side, the tension of having him touch me was amplified.

His palm was warm against my back when he laid it right on the part that hurt. He was good at this kind of thing. Even through the pain, his touch felt amazing.

Getting busy with Aidan was not a good idea. Definitely not something I should be picturing in my mind. But it was hard to keep my wariness bolstered when he kept healing me.

Once most of the pain had faded, he removed his hand.

"That's the best I can do. You need a night to fully recover."

I shifted, feeling mild pain and pulling muscles, but I was a lot better. He was right—I'd have full mobility by tomorrow.

"Thanks," I said. "You'd be handy to have on my normal jobs."

He grinned. "What you do is the opposite of my usual thing."

"But think of how good you'd be at it. All that experience protecting valuables, you'd have no problem breaking in to get them."

"I'll think about it." He grinned, but I knew he was full of it. "Where to next?"

"East," I said. "To Norway. The scroll didn't go far."

"East it is."

The wind cut off our words on the ride back, so we didn't talk. Aidan confidently piloted the boat through the waves and pulled alongside the little dock. I hopped off, and he tossed me the rope. I tied the boat off to the cleat while he hid the key beneath the pilot's seat.

By the time we were back in the car, it was fully dark.

"We'll stay at my place tonight," Aidan said as he cranked the ignition. "You need to sleep to heal. If the scroll were farther away, we'd take the plane and sleep on it, but Norway is only a two-hour flight."

"What about the demons who were looking for it?"

"If that's what they were after, they didn't get the information they needed. And I don't want you going until you're healed."

He was right. Going into tombs at less than one hundred percent was just asking for it. Without my magic, I needed to be physically one hundred percent to make it through the enchantments.

And I really wanted to wash the demon blood off me. I was starting to smell weird, and it was grossly sticky.

"Your place is near here?" Though I wanted to look at him—I wanted to do that way too often lately—I kept my gaze on the moonlit countryside. Hills rolled in the distance, dotted with sheep whose white wool glinted in the moonlight. I knew we were probably pretty close to where he lived. I didn't have a great idea of the geography of Ireland, but I knew we were in the south, and when I'd raided the temple on his property yesterday, I'd been in the south.

"Yes." He turned onto a narrow lane that climbed upward. The car bumped over potholes and rocks. "Just down this road. That's another reason I chose to borrow Mack's boat. Conveniently located."

We pulled up to the house a moment later.

"I see you like the simple things," I said as I gazed at the enormous structure. It was all sleek glass and stone, modern, yet it blended with the landscape beautifully.

"It's all right," Aidan said as he climbed out.

He opened my door before I'd even touched it, because I was too busy staring at the house. When I climbed out, my dragon sense tingled. Somewhere far underground, there were treasures. The ones that I'd left behind during my temple raid yesterday.

"Is your house on a cliff?"

"Yes."

Made sense. I'd entered the temple through a gap in a cliff. That's why it had been so easy for him to feel the magical disturbance when the demon had gone nuts on me. He'd been right on top of me.

I needed to be better about my recon, it seemed.

"Come on," he said. "Let's get some dinner."

"Yes, please." This guy knew the way to my heart. I followed him into the foyer. Lights turned on as soon as he walked in the front door, illuminating a simple but beautiful foyer. The ceiling soared overhead, and a modern glass chandelier shed gleaming light on the wood floor. Maybe if I didn't put all my money into the holy trinity of boots, jackets, and weapons, I could live in a place a bit closer to this.

Nah. I liked my set-up.

"Pick any bedroom upstairs and get cleaned up. I'll get dinner on."

I waved a hand down my bloody front. Most of it wasn't even mine. "What? You don't like me like this?"

His gaze met mine, and there was more than humor in his eyes. Heat. "I'll take you however I can get you."

I swallowed hard. Oh, man. He was bringing out the big guns. Desire coiled within me. Though it was stupid, I wanted to take him up on it.

"I'm going to get that shower." I turned and ran up the stairs.

His low laugh echoed from below. It pissed me off and turned me on at the same time.

Idiot.

But I didn't know if I was talking about him or me.

CHAPTER SIX

When I finished with my shower—which took longer than expected because the freaking thing had eight shower heads, and I'd had to try every one—I called Nix on my comms charm.

"Well, Cass? What happened?" Her voice came through clearly.

"I didn't get the scroll. But I have a bead on its location. We'll get it tomorrow."

"Good." The relief was clear in her voice. "Because Dr. Garriso didn't know much. He said the scroll has been lost for at least three hundred years. When it was first stolen, the Order of the Magica and the Shifter Council sent out a search party. But they never found it. No one has heard about it since. It just disappeared."

"Weird."

"Yeah. I spoke to Del. She's almost done in Nicaragua. When I asked her about the Scroll of Truth, she didn't know anything either."

"No surprise. If she'd known there was a threat to us, she'd have told us."

"Yeah. Just figured I'd try. You never know what she's read about."

True. When she wasn't beheading demons, she was big into books. It was why she was our Seeker. Most of the treasures I hunted were written about in ancient scrolls and texts. They provided the information I needed to find them.

"How's everything else?" Nix asked.

"What else?"

"Uh, you're hanging out with a super-hot, super-powerful, super-rich dude—who we all like, by the way—and you can't think of what else I might be asking about?"

"Oh, yeah, that." I blew out a breath. "I mean, he's cool and all."

"Cool? Yeah, he's cool. I met him. Tell me something I don't know. Something good."

"Well, he's healed me twice. And he's funny." I thought back. Being with him made me happy. I barely knew the guy, but I was getting butterflies over him. Yet I was also afraid of his ability to sense what I was. It was whiplashy. I needed to get my head on straight.

"But he wants me to find this scroll," I said. "Which, I'll remind you, could totally spill our secret. And all that power you say he's got…well, yeah. He's got it, all right. He turned into a griffon today."

"A griffon? Whoa."

"Yeah. With that kind of power, it's easier for him to sense other supernaturals' power. Even if I don't want to use mine, I'm scared that if I hang out with him long enough, I'll be in a situation where I'm forced to use it and I'll reveal myself."

Nix sighed. When she spoke, her voice was grim. "Yeah. That's serious."

"Deadly."

"All right, well a girl can hope. I'd like you to get a life, you know. Date, meet a guy, all that."

"Uh, like you do?" We kept to ourselves because of our secret and our work. Connor and Claire didn't know we were FireSouls, and they were our only real friends. With survival and running our business being our priority, dating hadn't been on our agenda much.

"Yeah, yeah. I see your point," Nix said. "Look, take care of yourself, all right?"

"I will. I'll be back soon. Remember—if I show up with the scroll, be ready to duplicate it real quick. Otherwise, I'm going to destroy it." Then I would have Aidan to deal with.

"I'll be ready."

"Miss you."

"Back at you," she said.

I reached up and tapped the silver charm with my finger, dimming its magic, then followed my nose toward something delightful.

On my way, I peeked my nose into an elegant family room and an enormous library, but it wasn't hard to find the kitchen. I'd been grateful not to see any food laid out in the elegant dining room that I'd passed before I'd reached the kitchen. Fancy dining rooms weren't really my natural habitat.

"How do you feel about pasta?" Aidan asked as I walked into the bright kitchen. It was all gleaming white and stainless steel, and even though nice kitchens weren't really my thing either, I couldn't help but like it.

My gaze landed on the big bowl in the middle of the kitchen table. There was salad and bread too, but it was the noodles tangled up with veggies and sausage that really got my attention.

"Fabulous," I said as I met his gaze. His hair was wet. "You managed to take a shower and make all this?"

He grinned—damn, I wished I could get over how good he looked when he grinned—and said, "I can't claim credit for the pasta. There's a housekeeper. Iona. She lives in the cottage out back. She made it but had to get back in time for her TV show."

"Well, thank her for me next time you see her, because this looks amazing." I sat down and reached for the pasta and piled my plate high. I didn't even bother to look at the salad, not when all this Italian goodness needed a home.

"Pasta fan?" Aidan asked as he sat down.

"You don't even know." The first bite was divine. Al dente noodles, rich sausage, flavorful veggies, and the sharp bite of some kind of cheese. Gorgonzola? "Heaven."

I plowed into the food.

"How exactly are you able to find the artifacts?" Aidan asked after a few bites.

I glanced up, my mouth full. I swallowed and got ready to deliver my spiel. "I have a bit of Seeker blood. My mom's side."

"That's strange," Aidan said. "Seekers usually don't have other powers. And you're a Mirror Mage, too?"

That part actually was true. I found that hiding lies with the truths helped. "Yep. A weird combo, but it works for me."

"I've never met a Seeker. How do you find the artifact?"

"Yeah, Seekers are rare." From my research, I knew that Seekers found artifacts basically the same way I did, so at least I could tell the truth. "I've never met another either. For me, when an artifact is far away, I get a feeling for its general location. Like I have a map inside me. It's kinda hard to explain."

"Try."

"All right. Once I have a general idea—like Norway—I go there. When I'm closer to the artifact, I get a better idea. I keep narrowing it down. Eventually, it's like I have a string tied around my waist that pulls me there."

I shut my mouth abruptly. I'd never shared that much detail with anyone before. Glossing over was more my style. What was it about him?

"What about you?" I asked, hoping to distract him. "You turned into a freaking griffon today. But you're more than just a shifter."

"Just a shifter? I'm *the* shifter."

I grinned. "Oh, so now you're cocky about it."

He grinned, not embarrassed. "It's the truth. It's hardly bragging if it's true. And I want you to like me."

"Ah…" I did not know how to deal with flirty Aidan. "So, you're *the* shifter. And you have powers you're hiding. Big powers. Even a weak mage like me can feel them. What are you, exactly?"

"That's a bit forward." He smiled.

I shrugged. It was a slightly rude question, but I didn't care. There wasn't a lot of outright fighting or warfare anymore—it was the modern age, after all—but supernaturals had a long history of duking it out with their magic. In any kind of fight, you had an advantage if no one knew your gifts or weaknesses. Hence everyone's silence on the matter, and Aidan's interest in getting the Scroll of Truth.

"Come on, impress me," I said. He already had, though. He was a griffon, for magic's sake. And he'd more than proven himself in the fight today.

"Shifter and Magica," he said.

So it was true. A hybrid. The first I'd ever met. No one knew how it happened. A Magica having a baby with a shifter wouldn't do it. The baby always turned out shifter, same species as the parent. That was hereditary.

"And you're the Origin," I said.

He shrugged. "The real Origin died millennia ago. She was my great-grandmother about six hundred times back. She was the real first shifter. I have her gifts, but I'm not the actual Origin."

"But you still go by the name."

"It's good for business."

"Which is?"

"Security. Origin Enterprises guards things that people want guarded. There's also an imports and exports division, specializing in things of value. And bodyguards."

"So you protect things, and I steal them."

"You're the shifty one in this pair." He indicated both of us.

"Hey, my operation is legal." Primarily because I stayed away from human artifacts and put back the magical ones that I found. "You really want to go on a date with me? I figured you'd want to stay away from slumming with the likes of me."

"You're interesting," he said. "I'd heard of you before. Anyone in the security business keeps up with the people who're experts at breaking and entering. But it wasn't until I met you that I realized there's something different about you. You're a Mirror Mage?"

"Yeah." I tried to keep my face expressionless. He didn't need to know the extent of my power. Or what I was.

"So that's how you get past the enchantments that protect the tombs."

"Exactly." Being a Mirror Mage allowed me to easily break the enchantments that protect temples and tombs. Because I could reflect back any kind of magic I came into contact with, I was perfectly suited to understanding and breaking enchantments. Fighting fire with fire.

Except the reality was that I used my wits and strength most of the time because my magic was so damned uncontrollable.

"Except I didn't sense any magic when I went down to the tomb after you broke in," he said.

"I'm not a very powerful mage, so I don't leave a lot of trace. And I don't use it often. It's more fun to go all Lara Croft on a place."

"Lara Croft?"

"*Tomb Raider*? Badass chick who's strong and smart and gets by on her wits?"

He grinned. "Yeah, I see it."

I relaxed a bit, hoping I'd thrown him off the scent. "What kind of Magica are you? Weather witch? Transport mage?" I asked to distract him. And I wanted to know.

He shot me a suspicious look, as if he knew I was trying to change the subject. Okay, so I wasn't going to get off that easy with him. Distraction was my chosen method of keeping people from asking questions, but Aidan struck me as the still-waters-run-deep kind of guy. Which was a good thing if you were looking for a date—but not if you were trying to keep a secret. He might act like nothing was up and he wasn't suspicious, but the look in his eyes made goosebumps pop up on my skin. I couldn't identify it.

Finally, he answered my question. "A variety."

My lips parted in surprise. "More than one?"

That was rare. Most Magica were born with one root gift. He was the Origin and a multi-gift Magica? That was off the charts.

"Yes," he said. "Go on a real date with me, and I'll tell you what they are."

I leaned back. "I can figure them out for myself, thanks. I'll just let you take on the baddies in whatever temple or tomb this scroll is hidden in. Then I'll see what you've got."

"Maybe it'll work. Don't count on it though." He grinned and it made those damned butterflies start flapping around in my stomach again.

Being around him was getting to be too much. He was too much. Too hot, too powerful, too wealthy. Worse, he was too much in the ways that mattered. He was nice, smart, and funny.

And he seemed to actually like me.

Nope, I could not handle this. It was way outside my pay grade.

I shoved the last bite of pasta into my mouth and pushed away from the table. "I've got to hit the hay. I'm exhausted. We'll leave early tomorrow?"

He nodded. "6 a.m."

"Great."

I headed back to the room I was borrowing and collapsed into bed. As I fell asleep, I realized that the expression I hadn't at first recognized on his face was one that should have made me nervous.

It was patience. As if he knew I had a secret and would wait to figure it out. Or, like he wanted to get to know me.

There was no way I could let that happen.

The helicopter hovered over the glittering water of the fjord, its rotors beating in the wind. The noise roared in my ears as the bright sun shone through the glass windows.

We'd flown to Bergen, on Norway's west coast, this morning and picked up a helicopter at the same airport. I had to admit, my job was a lot easier when the way was paved by Aidan's influence and money.

Norway's green mountains and glittering fjords spread out beneath us. I'd used my dragon sense to lead us here, following the pull of treasure at the other end of the line. Our pilot, Neilson, had followed my ambiguous directions to a T. She was in her sixties and had chin-length brown hair, cool sunglasses, and nothing fazed her. In short, she was the perfect helicopter pilot.

Aidan and I were strapped into the back. I squinted down at the forest below. It sat in the middle of a valley that ran perpendicular to the fjord. A river poured from it, feeding the massive body of water between the cliffs. The familiar strong tug of recognition pulled at my middle, directing me toward the valley.

"There!" I pointed below. "We need to land there."

"There's nothing down there!" shouted Neilson over the rotors.

"Just put us down," Aidan said.

"You'll have to use the ropes," Neilson said. "Nowhere decent to land."

"Not a problem," I said.

On the plane ride over, Aidan and I had discussed the possibility. Because of Norway's steep terrain, helicopter was the best way to scout for the site. But since landing a helicopter on a mountain wasn't always possible, we'd planned on a mid-air descent. Aidan had offered to jump out of the plane first and turn into a griffon so that I could jump onto his back. While it sounded totally badass, and I'd almost taken him up on it, it also sounded way to intimate. No way was I riding on his back.

So we were going the old-fashioned way.

Neilson hovered the helicopter over the trees about forty feet from the ground. Once it was stable—relatively—she shouted, "Whenever you're ready!"

Aidan and I glanced at each other and nodded, then turned to our separate doors on either side of the chopper. I pulled mine open and braced myself against the wind that whipped at my hair. My eyes watered. With my heart in my throat, I looked down.

Forty feet. Not so bad.

Enough to splat, but that was unlikely. At least, that's what I had to tell myself. I grabbed the hook and cable near the door and latched it to the harness I was wearing.

"Ready?" Aidan shouted against the wind.

I met his gaze. "Yeah!"

"Watch out for the trolls!" Neilson added.

Of course there would be trolls.

We both crouched at our door. With one last look at his ridiculously handsome face—I was weak, what could I say?—I lowered myself out of the helicopter. My weight on the rope made the gears kick in and it slowly lowered me to the ground. The wind buffeted me. Hell of a ride.

When my feet touched down, I unhooked my harness. Aidan did the same. We stood in the middle of a sparse forest, the narrow-trunked pine enveloping us.

With a wave, Neilson took off. We'd call her when we needed to get back out.

"You good?" Aidan asked.

"Better than." I closed my eyes and focused on the tugging sensation at my middle. "We're close."

"Good," Aidan said. "Because something is coming our way."

My ears perked up. There was a rumbling in the forest, as if something huge were running at us. I hadn't noticed it because I'd assumed it was the noise of the chopper flying away. Wrong.

I met Aidan's gaze. "Trolls."

Neilson hadn't been joking. Some parts of Norway had a bit of a troll problem. They were huge. Fifteen feet tall on average and weighed about two thousand pounds. I'd never actually seen one, but I knew they liked to hang out around ancient sites.

"Follow me." I set off through the forest, dodging tree trunks and jumping rocks. We were so close I could feel it. I assumed it was an ancient ruin of some kind, so we just had to get inside. If it was too small for the trolls to enter, they likely wouldn't destroy it. They had too much respect for the ancient sites.

Getting out would be a problem, but we'd deal with that when the time came.

Water sounded in the distance, which increased the likelihood someone had once built something here.

"We're close!" I shouted at Aidan, who ran at my side.

Suddenly, the trees thinned. Nothingness loomed before me. I skidded to a halt and looked down. A waterfall poured into a crystal pool about twenty feet below. The water sparkled, blue and inviting, surrounded by boulders and ferns. It looked deep enough to jump into.

"Oh no," I breathed.

"Where is it?" Aidan asked.

The thunder of the trolls chasing us grew louder.

"In there!" I pointed to the pool.

"What do you mean?"

I freaking hated this part. That water was going to be icy. "It's the entrance."

"So we jump?"

I liked that Aidan took it in stride. I personally wanted to bitch and moan for a little longer. Swimming in my boots sucks, but there was no way I'd leave them behind.

But I ran out of time. A roar ripped through the forest, and I looked back to see two trolls burst from the trees. They were well over fifteen feet tall and looked like they were made of stone. As if the mountain had come alive and spit them out. They each carried an enormous club.

"Jump!" I threw myself off the cliff, my stomach threatening to leap out of my mouth. Wind whipped by as I plummeted. I crashed into icy cold water.

Pain.

It was so cold my muscles froze up, and a pounding headache speared through my head. I kicked for the surface.

When I burst through, Aidan was beside me, his dark hair plastered to his head.

"Where to now?" he asked.

"Below. Swim down and look for a hole in the rock, probably. Then swim along until we get inside." Inside what, I wasn't sure. But I'd been in three tombs like this before, and I hoped this would be the same. My job didn't involve a whole lot of certainty.

The trolls above roared and I flinched. I treaded water and glanced up. They leaned over the cliff, glowering at us. Their roar made the leaves on the trees tremble.

"We can—"

The trolls leapt, crashing to the ground beside the pool. They'd jumped! I knew they couldn't swim—rock sinks, after all—but they had long enough arms that they could grab us.

"Now!" I sucked in a breath and dove, the icy water enveloping me. It was beautiful and blue as I swam down, kicking as hard as I could. A dark patch in the rock caught my eye, and I swam for it, praying the tunnel wasn't too long.

I grabbed a rock near the tunnel entrance and pulled myself toward it. There was only blackness beyond. It led into the mountain. This was it.

Aidan swam beside me, but he let me go in first. I kicked forward, my lungs burning and my boots making me slow. I really needed to practice my breath-holding. For a treasure hunter, this was pathetic. Lara Croft would be ashamed of me.

The tunnel was only about four feet in diameter. *Don't think about the size.* Tight spaces had never gotten me before. I hated them but I always won. I kicked and pulled myself along the rocks—anything to reach the end.

But the end wouldn't come. It was still dark and closed in. My lungs were on fire. If I wasn't halfway there by now, I was dead.

I scrambled around, ready to retreat. My number one rule in cave swimming—if you only have half your breath left but can't see the end, abort. It's your only chance at living.

I pushed at Aidan, expecting him to turn and swim back out. He didn't move. Fear surged in my chest. I wanted to scream at him. Though I knew I could make him hear me through the water, I couldn't let go of my air like that. I kicked myself forward, pushing. I couldn't get around him—there wasn't enough space. Didn't he know my lungs were smaller than his?

Suddenly, he pushed me forward. Panic clawed at me. I fought him, but he pushed me faster. I was flying through the water, completely disoriented.

Was I going up? What was—?

I broke the surface and sucked air into my burning lungs. It was dark all around me. My heartbeat thundered in my ears, deafening in the dark. Where was Aidan? I fumbled in an inner pocket of my jacket and pulled out a charmed lightstone. I shoved the ring onto my finger. It was too clunky to wear as jewelry, but the addition of the ring band made it easy to carry in situations like this.

I relied a lot on charmed objects like these. When I held it up, its glow illuminated the giant cave. An underground lake with a domed ceiling of stone soared above.

I spun, then jerked back, splashing. A creature with a smooth head and narrow snout looked at me.

Holy crap, a sea lion. A haze of gray light obscured the sea lion's head. When it faded, Aidan treaded water in its place.

"Seriously? A sea lion?" My voice echoed in the cavern.

"I don't like becoming a fish." He shuddered. "The gills."

"For magic's sake!" I shouted. "You weirdo. You scared the crap out of me!"

"We didn't exactly have a chance to talk about our plan back there."

"Yeah, I thought I was going to drown!" I splashed him, then kicked off for the ledge of rock at one side of the pool.

"There were trolls at the other end."

"I'd rather fight a couple trolls than drown," I wheezed as I pulled myself out of the water. "Then I could have gone and rented scuba tanks like a normal person. How did you even know there was an exit?"

"Once I changed, I could sense it." He heaved himself gracefully out of the water and stood beside me. I ignored him as I stomped my feet and shook myself off. I patted the knives at my thighs, grateful to find them still there. Though I collected loads of weapons, these were my favorites. The others were more like art to me. These were my workhorses.

"I'm sorry I scared you," he said.

I scowled at him. But he did look genuinely contrite. And we had made it down here.

"Fine. Just next time you're going to push me deeper into an underwater cave, warn me first." I shivered. "Freaking freezing in here."

"I know how to warm you up," he said. His gaze was hot enough to heat me to my core.

"If you're going to say body heat, don't even think it." But he'd made *me* think it.

"The offer's there."

Yes. I really wanted to take him up on it. *No, idiot.* I shook the tempting thought away. No matter how good he looked—and with his shirt plastered to his muscled chest, he looked really good—that was a bad idea. He was a powerful mage. He was the freaking Origin. If he hung out with me too long, he'd eventually sense what I was.

I'd have to ditch him as soon as this job was over. More than likely, I'd have to destroy the scroll as well. How I was going to do that without him noticing, I wasn't sure. But I'd figure it out when I got to it.

I dragged my mind away from that miserable thought and looked around the cavernous space. Shivers wracked me, but as with everything that scared me, I tried to ignore it.

"If you're not going to take advantage of my kind offer of body heat, let me at least dry you off the boring way," Aidan said.

My gaze darted to his. "The boring way?"

He held out a hand, and a flame burst to life in his palm.

"A Fire Mage," I said. They were strong. Suspicion hit me. "All four?"

"Yes."

Whew. Figured he could control earth, wind, fire, and water. That was super rare. Someone who could control all four was called an Elemental Mage. There were probably only a few in the world.

Was there anything average about this guy?

"But not all are equally strong," he added. "Fire and water are my strengths."

"Yeah, yeah. You're a freaking weakling. Thank god I'm not in a cursed temple with you as backup." I edged closer to the flame he held in his hand. It was warmer than a normal flame, and I could feel it drying my clothes.

"You know, you could just use your powers and duplicate this." He nodded at the flame.

"Why, when I can let you do all the work?"

"True. But I can feel your powers. You're not as weak as you say you are."

"But I'm lazy," I said, my heart starting to race. He could feel my power, at least the strength of it. But he hadn't mentioned feeling that I was a FireSoul. I latched onto that hope.

Was I going to have to use some of my powers around him just to convince him that I wasn't hiding something? But if I did, I'd blow something up for sure.

I shrugged off my jacket, which was probably ruined, and turned so that the flame could dry my back. It was a quick process, and the heat of the flame soon moved lower.

"Are you drying my butt?"

"It looked cold," Aidan said.

It was, so I decided to ignore how close his hand was to my rear and focus on getting dry. I also tried to ignore the tingling low in my belly, but I wasn't as good at that.

When I was mostly dry—save for my feet—I turned back around and searched the dark, holding up the hand that wore the lightstone. I could make out most of the cavernous space—three sides, with the fourth still in darkness. We stood on a ledge that extended to the right, into the dark. The rest of the cavern was flooded. The water was dark and murky. Sea monster water.

"I am so not looking forward to getting back into that," I said. I glanced at Aidan. "But next time, could you turn into a dolphin? I've always wanted to swim with dolphins."

"I'm not a petting zoo."

"I didn't say I'd pet you." Damn. That sounded dirty.

"Now that you put it that way, I could turn into a dolphin."

I scowled to cover my laugh then turned and set off down the rock ledge. My dragon sense was pulling me that way, and I was grateful for it. Aidan joined me.

Soon, my light illuminated three long shapes on the water. I squinted through the dark and approached slowly.

"Boats," Aidan said.

"Viking boats." I took in their sleek symmetry. There were three, their sides shallow and low to the water, the bows and sterns curved gracefully up in S-shapes. They were beautiful. I might have stolen ancient magic for a living, but I couldn't help but respect the amazing things that were created hundreds of years before I was born. Whenever I wasn't raiding or shopping online, I liked to read up on the history of the places I visited. "This design is at least a thousand years old. Viking."

"The monks did mention the Viking raids. But I didn't realize they meant the scroll."

"Neither did I.

"After a thousand years, the boats are still floating," Aidan said.

"Magic." We approached. There were no oars. "Definitely magic. This is how we get to the next part of the tomb."

"All right. Which one do you like?" he asked.

"The big one." We stepped on board. The deck was flat, but the boat was broad enough that it didn't rock much. I walked around, looking for anything that could ignite a spell that would propel the boat. A carving, a lever, anything.

There was nothing.

"Can you make the water move?" I asked. "Push us along?"

"You can't do anything?"

"I could, but I want to save my strength."

He looked at me suspiciously. "I thought there was something odd about how you don't use your power, but now I know there is."

"You're imagining things. Now let's get going."

"I'm not," he said. "And I'll get you to tell me what your deal is."

Not in this lifetime.

I glanced pointedly at the water. It swelled slightly behind the stern, pushing us along.

"Thanks," I said.

The boat drifted along the ledge as I walked to the bow. I held out my lightstone. It illuminated a dark tunnel entrance ahead of us. We glided beneath it. The air smelled staler, the fresh water and stone scent of the cavern fading.

I shined the light on the tunnel walls. Intricate carvings of swirls and knots decorated the space. Carvings of dragons swirled amongst them. Viking, definitely.

Something bumped the boat. I stumbled.

Another bump, this one harder. The water on the port side sloshed, and I peered into the murky depths. My heart pounded as I waited.

The boat careened as something huge crashed into it.

CHAPTER SEVEN

Aidan leaned over the side and peered into the water. "Sea monster."

I looked over in time to see a scaled back pierce the surface of the water, gliding sinuously along with us. Shiny silver scales glinted in the dim light.

"Do you think they're—"

Two hard bumps threw me to the deck. The bow swerved right. One of Aidan's waves rose up and pushed us back on course before we crashed into the stone wall.

Icy water splashed me from above, and the scent of rotten fish made me gag. I tilted my head back. A gaping mouth filled with dagger-teeth was crashing down upon me.

I rolled, scrambling along the deck. The sea monster's upper half hit the deck and slithered back into the water, bringing with it a chunk of the caprail.

So they were going for blood.

I climbed to my feet.

"My magic woke them," Aidan said.

"Yeah."

A huge head broke the water, razor sharp teeth flashing and blind eyes seeking. The monster plowed into the bow. Wood splintered and cracked.

I pulled my knives from their sheaths.

The grotesque head surged along with the boat, teeing up for another head-butt. I flung Righty at the sea monster's blind eyes. The obsidian drove deep into one milky orb. The creature thrashed and hissed, falling back into the water and sending up a wave that rocked the boat and splashed me with icy water.

Quickly, I nicked the back of my hand with Lefty. A second later, Righty flew out of the water, and I snagged it out of the air. I glanced at the tall, curving bow to see if we were taking on water. The wood was splintered several feet above the waterline, but we didn't seem to be taking on much water, if any.

Another bump crashed into the stern, nearly sending me to my ass again.

I turned to see another sea monster falling back into the water.

"Make us go faster. I'll hold them off," I said.

A deep green sea monster lunged out of the water, its gaping jaws aimed for my face. I flung Righty again. It pierced the skull of the beast, and it crashed beneath the surface.

I swiped my blade over the blood on the back of my hand and caught Righty when it flew back to me.

Aidan turned to the stern and directed his hands toward the water. Blue light flowed from his palms, and his magic prickled over me, at once disturbing and pleasurable. The waves that pushed us grew, and the boat shot forward.

A sleek, scaled back raced alongside us, aiming for the bow. I threw my blade at it. The shining obsidian landed in the monster's neck, but the thing kept surging forward. They were so big I had to land a headshot. I called Righty back as I flung Lefty, this time nailing the beast between the eyes. The sea monster thrashed and sank beneath the surface. I called my blade back.

Thank magic my blades were so sharp. Since I refused to use my own power, I'd be up a creek without my enchanted tools.

My heart pounded in my throat as I waited for more. It was eerily silent, just the sound of the waves lapping at the tunnel walls. The bow cut smoothly through the water, carrying us farther into the dark.

"I don't sense them anymore," Aidan said.

I nodded. "There may have only been three."

It was a good number for magic, though I wasn't sure why. Enchantments and protections sometimes came in groups of three because of it.

A shiver shook me. "It's getting colder."

"And the magic is thicker," Aidan said.

He was right, and it was the kind I didn't like. It prickled over my skin like gnat bites. The scent of rotting fish didn't fade. I'd been wrong—it wasn't the scent of the sea monsters. It was dark magic. The kind that was meant to harm, not just protect the treasures within this place.

I sure hoped whoever had created this place was dead.

I moved to the bow, holding out my light. There was nothing ahead of us but more tunnel. At least it was silent. The journey was tense, but the tunnel eventually widened into another cavern. This one was smaller, but there was another stone ledge to climb out at.

And another boat.

As Aidan steered our vessel alongside the dock, I jumped onto the stone ledge and ran to the other boat. It was empty, but the deck was wet.

"I don't think we're the only ones here," I said. My heart beat against my ribs. This was bad. Were they after the same thing we were? I couldn't let anyone else get ahold of it.

Aidan tied our boat to a stone pillar and came to my side. "I agree. I thought I smelled blood in the water before the first sea monster attacked our boat."

"You can smell that well?" I asked.

"It was a lot of blood."

Great. "Let's go then."

Only one tunnel led away from the water, so we followed it. I hurried ahead, holding my lightstone aloft and moving as quickly as the uneven ground would let me. My belly churned at the idea that someone else might have the scroll.

Fortunately, the tunnel was narrow and short, opening up to an enormous cavern.

"Whoa." I tilted my head back to take it in. "It's like the Super Dome."

"With obstacles," Aidan said. He'd walked ahead of me and created a ball of flame that he'd sent high into the air to illuminate what my light could not.

I joined him.

The ground dropped away in front of us. "Oh, crap."

An enormous pit stretched out ahead, piles of stone dotting it all the way to the other side, where it rose up to a cliff that was the same level as ours. The eerie orange light of Aidan's flame set the rocks aglow.

"I've seen this before," I said. "In Myanmar. The piles of rock down there used to be towers. You jump across them, but if you don't know the pattern, they collapse." I squinted down into the pit. "I don't see any bodies. Maybe they were demons. Or they made it across." I hoped they hadn't.

Aidan rubbed a hand over his chin. "I'll take us across."

"You? As in, griffon you? I thought shifters didn't like carrying people."

"Normally, we don't." His gaze met mine. "But you're an exception."

There was something in his gaze that made me nervous. In a good way. More anticipation than nerves.

It was heat, I realized.

And I liked it.

I swallowed hard, then glanced down at the pit. It was a bad idea to ride on Aidan's back. I knew it was. It wasn't like I had a thing for griffons or anything. That'd be way weird. But I was starting to accept that I had a thing for Aidan.

It wasn't the physical part of riding a shifter that was intimate. It was the connection. They were willingly letting you into their magic sphere. It was intangible, but you got to know them better. Like a window into their magic and their mind.

But we didn't have time to climb down. We had to reach whoever was ahead of us before they got the scroll.

"Unless you want to use your gifts and shift with me?" he asked.

Oh, crap. If I did that, I'd probably turn into the biggest, most powerful griffon ever. Then fall out of the air because I couldn't use my wings.

Not good.

"I'm too weak to shift. I can mirror other magic, but not shifting." At least it was true that shifting was harder. I'd tried to turn into a house cat once. It hadn't been pretty.

I pasted a smile onto my face. "I'll take you up on that ride. We need to catch up to whoever is here."

His dark gaze snared mine. I forced myself not to look away.

"I don't think I believe you," he said. "But that's for another day."

I tried to control the shuddery breath of nervous relief that escaped me. "Okay, let's do this."

In a flash of silvery gray light, Aidan transformed into an enormous griffon. His coat shined gold in the light of the flame overhead. It glinted off his enormous, powerful wings. I'd bet it took a lot of magic to keep a flame going while not in human form.

My fingers itched to touch the silken feathers that covered his wings, and I clenched my fists. I met his black gaze, trying to figure out if I could see Aidan inside him. His great beak sent a shiver of fear through me. It could crush my chest like a twig. So could his claws, which were huge and spiked.

I'd once thought dragons had to be the scariest mythical creature. I'd been wrong. It was griffons.

And I was damn glad this one was on my side.

For now, at least.

Griffon-Aidan knelt before me so I could climb onto his back. His fur was soft and warm—hot almost—and I scrambled up on top of him.

A sense of power rushed over me, as if I were being enveloped in his magical strength. It felt like my memories of using my own power. I'd cut myself off from that for so long that I'd forgotten how good it felt the few times I'd used it. Like I was in control of my life and could do anything.

Life right now was all about rolling with the punches—many of which landed. If I had my own power, I could control my destiny. I could take what I wanted. *Be* what I wanted.

But this was just a connection with his power. It wasn't my own.

It could be, though. I could unleash what was within me and mirror what he had. I could also have this strength. I had more than enough inherent power to mirror his magical gifts—more, if the legends about FireSouls are true. With practice, FireSouls could manipulate the gifts we stole, becoming the strongest of that gift. An ArchMage or ArchSorcerer of that gift.

Oh, that would feel good.

But I hadn't ever practiced my magic. The few times it had blasted out of me, I'd caused some serious damage. I couldn't do that again. Nor could I be caught. I'd put my *deirfiúr* at risk. And myself.

So I embraced the feeling of being connected to Aidan. I breathed in the forest scent of his magic as he pushed off from the ground and swept up into the air. The ground fell away beneath us as his powerful wings carried us toward the center of the cavern. The wind tore at my hair and clothes. Exhilarating.

But the best part was Aidan. It was like I could feel inside his mind. Not read his thoughts, but his feelings. His intentions. His aura.

I was enveloped in a sense of commitment. Loyalty and honor. All the good things people say when they talk about a hero. But it was more complex than that. He was more complex, but I couldn't put my finger on how. I was too distracted by the feeling of his power embracing me.

I tried to focus on my surroundings—on the eerie orange rocks flying by beneath me—instead of how good it felt to be with Aidan like this.

It was hard not to focus on his power and strength. I wanted to study it. Absorb it.

When he touched down on the other side, I scrambled off as fast as I could. I could hardly catch my breath and stumbled.

"Damn." I wasn't normally so clumsy. Being sure on my feet was key to surviving my job.

A strong hand caught my shoulder and steadied me. I turned. Aidan was already human again, a testament to his strength. So were the clothes. He never appeared naked like some shifters.

"Are you all right?" His deep voice washed over me like a warm ocean wave. His dark eyes met mine.

"Yeah. Just the flying." *Liar.*

He pulled me closer and my skin sparked. But it wasn't his magic. It was just him making me lose my mind. It was becoming hard to breathe.

"Are you sure?" His voice was low, his gaze hot. He loomed over me.

I nodded but couldn't speak.

His gaze dropped to my lips.

Oh no, was he going to kiss me?

His lips looked so good—full and warm.

Do it.

His forest scent wrapped around me, drawing me closer. His magic caressed me, stroking over my skin like silk. When his big hand squeezed my shoulder lightly, I leaned into it, relishing his strength.

His power surged, as if he liked me leaning on him. He was a predator—of course he liked it when his prey gave in.

The thought shocked me into action. I pulled away. Not only was this a bad idea, we weren't the only ones here.

"Let's go," I said. "Whoever came before us is probably already in the tomb."

He pulled me to him. "You wanted that too."

The desire surged again, making my breath come short. "I don't know what you're talking about."

"A kiss." His husky voice sent a shiver across my skin.

"I didn't."

113

He grinned. He was so handsome I almost hated him. How was I supposed to resist that? Especially after everything I'd felt while we were flying?

"Liar," he said "But you're right. Now isn't the time."

"Never is the time." I spun and raced toward the exit, eyeing the ground in front of me for anything suspicious. Normally I didn't run through enchanted places like this unless I had to, but whoever came before us would have probably tripped any enchantments, so I took the risk.

Once again, the tunnel was an exit. I hoped like hell that the next cavern was our destination.

Aidan was close behind me, but even his forest-fresh scent couldn't drown out the smell of rotten fish in the air. It was getting stronger. The lightstone illuminated carvings on the tunnel walls, even more than before. We were getting closer. I couldn't look carefully as I ran, but I could make out writing, maps, images. Weird.

A chill in the air washed over me, more than the normal cold. The smell of ice and snow froze my nose.

"You feel that?" Aidan asked.

"Yeah." And it was disturbingly familiar. Fear hit me, acid and sharp. "Phantoms."

Silvery light drifted out from the walls, coalescing into the ghostly forms of men draped in cloaks. More monks? They shimmered so that it was hard to make out their features, but that didn't matter. You didn't need to see them—they only needed to see you.

"Try to protect your mind," I said, as I ran faster. "You can't fight Phantoms. They create nightmares inside your head."

Second to being tossed in the Prison for Magical Miscreants, I was most afraid of Phantoms. I tried to build a steel cage around my mind as I ran, but I knew it wouldn't work. There were too many. They stood along the tunnel walls on either side, stretching as far as my eye could see.

"Intruders," they whispered.

"Thieves," they hissed.

"FireSoul."

They reached out with silvery hands, clawing for me but not leaving their place at the wall. Phantoms couldn't touch you, but they didn't need to. The pain hit me as they went for my mind. The cold tendrils of their dark magic reached inside my head, weaseling through my brain. I stumbled as the pain pierced me like an icepick through the eye.

They were going for my worst memories, but they didn't know that those were hidden from me by the pain that welled every time I tried to uncover them. My stomach lurched at the torture, and I nearly vomited as they pushed harder inside my head. I stumbled to my knees. Aidan's big hands lifted me to my feet. He started to pick me up, but even through my pain, my stubbornness surged.

I took care of myself or I wasn't Cass Clereaux. I didn't know my past self—I wasn't about to lose my present self as well. Sweat dampened my skin as I ran, trying to get past the Phantoms as quickly as possible.

The worst of the pain was fading as the Phantoms abandoned my memories in favor of my fears. An image of my *deirfiúr* being thrown into the Prison for Magical Miscreants tore through my mind. The cell was dank and dark and the iron bars thick.

Horror lurched in my belly, but at least the pain had faded enough that I could run. If I'd slowed, I knew that Aidan would have thrown me over his shoulder.

My lungs burned as we raced down the corridor, our feet pounding on the stone. The rancid air that I sucked into my lungs tasted foul, but I needed it. Even Aidan's breathing sounded loud beside me.

Darkness loomed ahead, and gratitude welled within me. No glowing silver light meant no more Phantoms lining the walls.

We burst through into a small, dark chamber and stumbled to a halt, panting.

"Why did they keep saying traitor?" Aidan asked, leaning on his knees.

I glanced up at him from my similar position. "Your worst memories or your greatest fears. It's their weapon."

I wondered if being a traitor was his worst memory or his greatest fear, but he was silent. I was just grateful he hadn't heard them saying FireSoul. Only I had heard that. Phantoms didn't speak the way humans did—they just reflected your fears back at you, using your mind. Though it was hell to be around them, I didn't have to worry about them spreading my secret because they didn't communicate normally.

"I'd bet the phantom monks built this place when they were alive," I said. "When they died, they stuck around as phantoms to protect it."

"What, they were a rival holy order that stole the scroll?"

"Yeah, maybe. All the carvings on the walls back there—that was just a compilation of collected knowledge. Maps, drawings, writing. Maybe they heard about the scroll and wanted to add it to their collection."

"So they stole it from the Irish monks." He nodded. "Makes sense."

"I think we're in an antechamber," I said as I looked around the room. It was dark and nearly empty. Two stone benches lined either wall, and there was a huge wooden door ahead of us.

I drew my daggers, then glanced at Aidan. He had no weapons—but then, he didn't need them. I approached the door.

"Ready?" I asked Aidan.

He nodded and I pushed open the left door.

"Ohh damn," I breathed.

Soaring shelves piled high with treasure filled the cavernous space. Gold, ivory, and precious stones blinked at me. Weapons and dishes and books and jewelry made from every precious substance known to man filled the enormous room. Covetousness surged within me. These weren't my usual treasures, but I could make space in my trove. I could clear out the leather jackets and books and fill it with everything that sparkled in this wonderland.

A terrifying roar startled me out of my stupor. I jumped. Beside me, Aidan had changed into a griffon, his wings and fur as golden as the treasures around me.

When I looked back at the room, I saw the demons for the first time. I'd missed them because of the gold. They scaled every shelf, crawling like giant spiders searching for something, though they had the normal number of limbs. There were more than a dozen of them, and all were man-shaped and dark gray. Were they looking for the scroll too?

Had to be. These were the individuals that Aidan's seer had prophesied to be looking for the scroll.

One turned and threw a blast of burning smoke at Aidan, who dodged it in mid-air.

Holy magic, they were shadow demons. Like the one who'd called me a FireSoul just the other day. I hadn't been sure if the ones on the monks' island were the same because they hadn't thrown smoke. Just looking similar didn't make them the same. But the smoke throwing sure as heck did.

Coincidence?

No way. I'd gone my whole life without someone calling me out on what I was. Now I'd seen them three times. Too many times to ignore.

They all had to die.

I charged into the room as Aidan launched himself into the air. His wings beat powerfully as he soared to the top of the shelves and pulled the demons off with his front claws. He tore them apart, a gruesome but efficient job.

The thud of bodies sounded around me.

There were three demons on the ground and they all turned to me. Mine. I flung Righty at one. It sunk deep into his neck. I called the blade back as the demon fell, then turned to another.

Just in time to see him pick up a golden orb that sat alone on a majestic pedestal in the middle of the room. It was the only piece of treasure not on a shelf.

He lifted it and aimed at Aidan.

"No!" I shouted.

The number one rule in tomb raiding—never, ever pick up something that sits alone on a pedestal. It always sets off a booby trap, and it's almost always of the giant rock variety. Hadn't he seen *Indiana Jones*?

'Course not. He was a demon. And now we were screwed.

A crack streaked across the ceiling like lightning. Aidan hovered in the air beneath, going for a demon that clung to one of the tall shelves. A second later, a boulder fell from the ceiling. Then another, straight onto Aidan. It hit him in the shoulder, knocking him out of the air.

His huge form plummeted, thudding to the ground. Rocks crashed around him. He didn't get up.

No! He was going to be crushed to death.

My magic flared to life. Blindly, I reached out for his gift, terrified.

I was risking my life for his, but I couldn't stop myself. If I didn't bring this whole place down with my uncontrollable power, he could figure out what I was.

I opened myself up to his magic, not even trying, and it crashed into me. Like the waves I'd heard when I'd first met him, it swamped me. Power flooded my senses, making my skin tingle and my head buzz. I grasped with my mind, trying to sort through the myriad of gifts that were now at my disposal. Fire, water, wind, rock. He could control them all.

I didn't know what to do—I'd never practiced—so I went on instinct. I dropped my knives and threw my hands out toward the falling rock, envisioning them flying away from Aidan. I poured everything into it, my will and hope and determination.

The rocks hurtled horizontally through the air, diverting themselves from the griffon. Boulders plowed into the walls, causing even more damage than they would have if they'd fallen, but at least Aidan was alive.

Sweat poured down my face as I kept up the stream of power. Breath burned in my lungs.

Finally, the rocks stopped falling. I dropped my hands and bent over, panting. Fortunately, we were inside a mountain, so the battered walls would still hold. I'd destroyed some of the bookshelves and hoped the scroll had been on one.

I only had a second to recover. It wasn't enough. Using that much magic was draining. I'd forgotten about the surviving demons. One plowed into my middle, throwing me to the ground.

Though I tried to fight back, I was weak from using my power.

Out of the corner of my eye, I saw Aidan rise to his feet. He launched into the air again, swooping down to pull the demon off me.

I scrambled up, more awkward than I'd ever been, and grabbed my blades. Another demon jumped out at me from behind a pile of rubble. Startled, I flung Righty at him. My arm was so weak that my aim was way off. It sunk into his shoulder, and he crashed to his back. I limped to him and straddled him, then grabbed the dagger plunged into his shoulder and twisted.

"What do you know?" I panted.

His black eyes met mine, and he just stared at me, as if the pain didn't affect him at all.

A blast of burning smoke slammed into me. I crashed to the ground beside the demon. He pulled my dagger from his chest, then scrambled up and toward the figure who'd blasted me.

I grabbed my blade and flung it at him. He collapsed. I staggered to my feet. Fates, I was so weak!

Out of the corner of my eye, I caught sight of Aidan tearing apart the demon who'd blasted smoke.

Good.

I swiped Lefty across the cut on the back of my hand, and Righty yanked itself out of the demon's chest, returning to me. I spun, looking for more prey.

The last demon stood in front of the soaring bookshelves.

I blinked. It wasn't a demon. It was a man. A Magica of some kind. I hadn't noticed him earlier, but he was definitely not a demon. I threw Righty at him. It sank into his shoulder.

Damn it! I was so tired I couldn't even throw straight.

I called the blade back to me. As it was pulling itself from his shoulder, he dug something out of his pocket and hurled it to the ground. A puff of glittering silver smoke wafted up, and he stepped into it.

As he disappeared, I saw the big ivory scroll gripped in his hand.

"No!" I reached out, but he was gone. At the last second, I snagged the blade that flew toward me.

The rest of the place was in chaos—rocks everywhere, golden objects glinting from every nook and cranny—but there were no more living demons. One lay on the ground, though.

Maybe he wasn't dead yet. I stumbled toward him as griffon-Aidan landed and transformed back into a man. The demon was sprawled on his back, his middle looking crushed. His face was a waxy gray. Aidan must have crushed him and dropped him, but he wasn't dead yet if he hadn't disappeared.

I smacked his face. "Wake up!"

He lay still.

I shook him by the collar. Nothing. All I seemed to be doing these days was shaking demons and trying to get them to talk.

Aidan knelt by my side and dug around in the demon's pockets.

"What are you doing?" I asked.

"He might have a transport charm. His buddy did." He pulled his hand out and showed me. A small rock. "Can you track him?"

I closed my eyes and reached out for the man who'd disappeared, even though I knew it was likely hopeless. I kept my hand on the unconscious demon's chest, but felt nothing.

"No," I said.

"I thought Seekers could track people."

They could, but Seeker was just my cover story. I could only find people or things of value. The demon at my feet didn't value his comrades, so there was no link for me. I valued finding the man I'd just seen, but I didn't know enough about him to track him. Or he was protected. Either way, I was getting nothing.

"I can't feel where he went. I don't know why," I said.

My shoulders sagged. What a crap day.

Black glass flashed in the light at the demon's side. My blades. I reached for one, then remembered. "Blood. I threw my blade at the man who disappeared. I called it back to me before he left. We can use the blood on the blade to fuel a tracking spell! That should be enough to find him."

I was pretty fastidious about washing the blood off my beloved blades, but I could wait if it meant finding the man who'd taken the scroll.

"Do you know where to buy a spell like that?" he asked.

It wasn't easy to buy magic that wasn't your own. It's why my business did so well—a lot of demand, little supply. "I don't, but I think my friends would. They know a lot of people. They've hooked me up with charmed objects in the past."

"Good. Let's go then." He stood.

I rose, swaying on my feet. Fates, using magic was hard. I was so out of shape.

"Are you all right?" Aidan steadied me.

Had he been conscious when I'd moved the rocks?

"Yeah, just beat up." And it would take me a while to get over the shock of using that much power.

"You look like you're a bit more than beat up."

"Nah, I'm fine. I totally—"

Wooziness hit me hard. I swayed on my feet. Right as I tipped over to go hang out with the floor, Aidan swept me up into his arms.

Wow, that was nice. Not only did I not have to support my own weight, but he was also warm and strong, and his arms felt heavenly.

"You're not all right," he said.

"Just tired. Put me down."

"No."

I scowled. "Fine. Let's go back. Potions & Pastilles."

Suspicion glinted in Aidan's dark eyes. "There's more to it than exhaustion."

"There isn't."

"So you didn't save my life from those rocks?"

Oh, crap. "I don't know what you're talking about."

He gave me a look that said he didn't buy my bull for a second.

"We'll talk about it later," he said, then threw the transport charm to the ground. It shattered and he stepped into the glittering cloud.

CHAPTER EIGHT

Fortunately, Potions & Pastilles was empty when we arrived. Because of the time change, we'd hit it right at the late-afternoon lull. Old Mr. Monier sat at his usual table in the corner, reading the paper, but he was deaf as a post, so I wasn't worried about him.

"Where do you want me to put you?" Aidan asked.

"Down," I said as Claire walked out of the back. She was dressed in her fighting leathers, either on her way to a job or just returning from one. I would guess returning, from the state of her hair. It looked like someone had gotten ahold of her ponytail and tugged.

"What's wrong with you?" Claire demanded. Her dark eyes searched me worriedly.

"I'm fine," I said.

"Yeah, 'cause you totally let people carry you around when you're fine."

"Just a little tired from a fight." I pushed at Aidan's chest. "Put me down!"

Gently, he lowered me to my feet. I stumbled. The ground felt like it was moving. Ugh, I was never using my power again. So not worth this feeling.

"Let me get you something," Claire said.

"I'll take a triple boosted latte," I said as I stumbled to the comfy chairs in the corner in front of the window. Potions & Pastilles specialized in enchanted coffees, courtesy of Connor's potions talents. Normally I drink the regular stuff, but if you're injured, magically drained, bummed out, or just looking for a boost, P & P had something to help you out. I didn't know what was in the boost that I'd just ordered, only that Connor specialized in righting your ills. Or at least, giving you a pick-me-up that had more to do with magic than caffeine.

I sank into the comfy chair and sighed. All I needed was a drink and a nap and I'd be fine.

Aidan sat down next to me, looking entirely too fit and healthy. There wasn't a scratch on him.

"You aren't a weak Mirror Mage," he said. "You lied."

My heart thudded. "You don't need to know everything about me. We're just doing this one job together. As long as I get it done, it doesn't matter how I do it."

"True. But I want this to be more than just one job."

We were getting right to it, then. "Can't we talk about this later?"

"Now's good."

"I'm not feeling great, as I'm sure you can see."

"Exactly. If I wait until your defenses are up, you'll just leave. I want to know why you don't use your power. After what you did with those rocks, I know you're strong."

"Strong? I made a mess." I winced at the memory. That would be hard to repair. Impossible, probably. But if I hadn't done it, Aidan might have died.

"Yeah, maybe. But you saved my life. It takes a lot of power to divert the path of thousands of tons of stone." His dark eyes turned serious.

"Can you just say thank you and forget it? Consider it a favor to me for saving your life."

His expression sobered. "You're right. Thank you. I didn't realize the ceiling was cracking until the boulder hit me. The place looked sturdy."

"It was. A dumb demon tripped the most obvious booby trap in the book."

Aidan quirked a brow, then grinned. "The golden orb on the pedestal."

"How'd you know?" I liked that he was so quick.

"I've seen Indiana Jones. And I noticed the orb when I went in. Then right before the boulder hit me, something gold flew by my head. He chucked it at me, didn't he?"

"Yeah."

"Idiot. But you saved my life."

"Which I might regret, if you don't lay off."

"Why are you hiding your strength?" His gaze searched my face.

"I thought you said that I was right and you were going to lay off."

"No. I said you were right that I owed you my gratitude. But I still want to know why you're hiding how strong you are. You're not a weak Mirror Mage."

"I was just never good with my magic, okay?" I said. "That's basically the same thing as being a weak Mirror Mage. I'm too weak to control it, so I don't like to use it."

"So practice."

"That's a little difficult when one destroys everything around them when they try." And I didn't want to be good with my magic—at least not as much as I wanted other things. Other supernaturals were always interested in knowing who was the best at what. I just wanted to have my nice little life full of adventure and my friends— I didn't need to be super powerful to have that.

"Didn't your parents train you?"

The question hit me like a blow between the eyes. I opened my mouth to answer, but nothing came out.

"Hey, I didn't mean—"

"Triple boosted latte, piping hot!" Claire said as she came out of the kitchen. Connor followed her with a plate and another cup.

I glared at Aidan, though my heart was pounding. I didn't want to talk about my parents. Hell, I didn't even know how to talk about my parents.

Aidan closed his mouth, but the look on his face was clear. This discussion wasn't over. He looked like he was sorry he'd brought up a subject that clearly made me uncomfortable, but also like he wasn't going to let go of it.

Just what I needed on top of feeling like I'd been run over by a truck.

"Thank you." Gratefully, I took the steaming cup from Claire and sipped it.

Warmth and strength flowed into me. Not enough to repair me fully, but I felt a bit better.

"Brought you one of the same," Connor said as he handed a cup to Aidan. "You don't look as beat as Cass, but you could probably use it. "

"Thanks," Aidan said.

"And some pasties." Connor put the plate of savory treats on the little table in front of our chairs. His apron was dusty with flour, but the rest of his clothes—jeans, a t-shirt, and Converse—were spotless.

"You're the best." I grabbed one, not caring that it was hot, and bit into it. My stomach was suddenly cavernous. I vaguely remembered being famished after I'd used my magic in the past. The pasty was so good I almost groaned.

"What's got you looking like you were dragged through a harpy nest?" Claire asked.

"Job gone wrong," I said around a bite of pasty. "We're looking for a tracking spell now."

"You can't get a read on something?" Connor asked.

I swallowed hard, the pasty suddenly a lump in my throat. Time to lie. They also thought I was a Seeker. I hated lying to my friends, but it protected them. They could get in trouble for knowingly harboring a FireSoul. If I were an actual good person, I'd probably stay away from them.

But I was weak. I liked my friends. And as long as I was careful, I could keep my secret and keep them safe.

"Yeah, this one is tough," I said. "Don't know why. Maybe the guy is using a concealment charm. Do you know anyone strong enough to make a tracking charm off a bit of blood?"

Connor and Claire looked at each other. They both had different contacts given that Connor stuck to potions and baking for a living, and Claire hunted bad guys and only occasionally helped out at P & P, but their circle of friends was wide.

"What about Mordaca?" Connor asked. "She's a Seeker, right?"

"The one you have the hots for?" Claire asked.

"That's the one." Connor grinned.

"She's scary, but yeah, she could probably do it." Claire met my gaze. "I've got one friend I can call. Give me a sec."

She got up and moved to the window, then pulled out her phone.

"Mordaca?" I asked Connor as Claire made the call.

"Yeah. Sexy Blood Sorceress with some Seeker talent like you. Bit scary like Claire said, but she could probably use her sorcery to make you a charm."

"Sounds perfect."

Claire returned a second later. "All right. She's in LA tonight, but she'll be back by morning. She said she should be able to make you a charm, but it'll cost you."

I glanced at Aidan, but I figured he was good for it.

He nodded once. "Thank you."

"Can't we meet her tonight? We can fly to LA."

"She insisted she was busy," Claire said.

"And you need to rest," Aidan said.

"I'm fine."

"Actually, you look like you're melting into a puddle," Claire said.

I glanced down at myself. Okay, yeah, my posture was so slumped that I might look like I was about to pass out. That coffee hadn't fixed me as much as I'd thought.

I turned to Aidan. "What if the guy who stole the scroll reads it?"

"For one, he might not be able to read old Irish. And if he did and poses a threat, we'll kill him."

The threat in his eyes was so real that I believed him. And he was right, I could barely walk. Without sleep, I'd be worthless. "Fine. We'll wait."

"Why are you so interested?" he asked. "You seem to be taking this more personally than a normal job."

My heart jumped into my throat. He couldn't be onto me. "I take all my jobs personally. That's why I'm the best."

"Uh huh," Aidan said, suspicion still in his eyes. He turned to Claire. "When do we meet Mordaca?"

"She said to meet her at eight at the Apothecary's Jungle in Darklane." Claire glanced at her cellphone. "I've got to run. A client is waiting on me."

"I thought you just finished a job?" I asked, glancing at her hair.

"Yep. Nasty Sorabug infestation at a rich guy's house over in Enchanter's Bluff."

"Ew." Sorabugs were gross. They were the size of ponies—hence the reason for hiring a mercenary instead of an exterminator—and had giant pincers. Even the nicest neighborhood in town wasn't immune to their gross invasions. Fortunately they stuck to magical cities or else humans would think aliens had invaded.

"Yeah, this job should be better. Protection detail for a visiting aristocrat," she said.

"Protection from what?"

"That's the thing—I'm not sure. And I don't like that."

It was that wariness that kept my friend alive. Claire was one of the best mercs in Magic's Bend. Mercenaries were hired for all kinds of jobs—not just killing. Though she did that too, as long as she thought the client deserved it. No kids or innocents. Our world was full of all kinds of dangerous jobs you could hire a mercenary for. It was Claire's selectiveness that kept her alive.

"Be safe," I said.

"Always." She grinned, then headed out the door, straightening her ponytail as she went.

A pair of pink-haired old ladies walked in after she left, no doubt out for a day of antiquing at the shops down the street from my own. Those antiques had no magical charms, however.

"Good luck with your tracking spell," Connor said as he went to help the women with their order.

I turned to Aidan. "I'm beat. I'm going to go get cleaned up and hit the hay. I'll see you tomorrow morning?"

"We have more to talk about." His voice was commanding.

"Not now, we don't." I stood, trying my damnedest not to sway. The last thing I needed was him carrying me down the street.

Aidan surged to his feet and put a steadying hand on my shoulder. "Fine, not now. Go rest. I'll see you later."

"Pick me up at seven." Though I wanted to try to beat him to Mordaca, it was highly unlikely that I could afford her fee.

We parted ways outside P & P. I had to insist that he not carry me back to my apartment, but by the time I walked in front of Ancient Magic, I was about ready to fall over. The door weighed a hundred pounds as I pushed inside.

Nix looked up from behind the counter. "Whoa, you look rough."

I leaned against the door. "I feel it. Will you help me up to my place?"

"Yeah. It's almost five. I'll just close up."

It only took her a second to grab her phone and her book, then she was at my side, her arm wrapped around my ribs.

"No luck with the scroll?" she asked as she locked the door. I leaned against the wall as she ran her hands around the edge, triggering the enchantment that would protect the shop from thieves while we were away.

"Not yet. I'll tell you about it up at my place."

The walk up the three flights of stairs felt like climbing the monks' island mountain again. By the time I got to the top, my lungs burned and my thighs ached.

"What the heck is wrong with you?" Nix asked as she dumped me on the sofa. "You've never been this weak. Did you get hit by something?"

"No spells. Unless you count my own."

"What do you mean?" Her eyes widened.

"I used my magic."

"What?" she gasped. "You're joking. Did Aidan see you?"

"Yeah." I buried my head in my hand. "I was an idiot."

Nix paced my small living rom. "No. You weren't. You haven't used your magic in ten years. You're careful. You must have had a good reason."

Her support warmed me. "I thought Aidan was going to die."

"That's a pretty good reason. Was he?"

"Yeah, maybe a sixty, seventy percent chance. Though it felt like more at the time. I freaked out." The memory of the rock hurtling toward him still gave me the shakes.

"You like him."

There was no question in her voice. To protect my *deirfiúr's* secret, I would let someone I didn't care for die—I'd kill to protect their secret. It was my secret too, but like with most things that involve a threat to oneself, it didn't feel quite as real. But the threat to them felt very real.

Apparently I cared enough for Aidan to try to save his life, even though it meant possibly revealing what we hid.

"I'm sorry," I said. My throat tightened with tears. I never cried. Not much was worse than waking up in a field as a kid with no memories and no parents. After that, tears seemed a bit silly.

"Don't be. We can take care of ourselves. And I have a good feeling about Aidan."

"Really? Because I don't."

"Yeah, you do." Nix looked at me like I was an idiot. "You saved him. You obviously have a good feeling about him."

"I did. But he knows something's up with me. He's suspicious of why I don't use my powers. And when I finally did use them, I overdid it. He knows I'm powerful. I'm afraid he's going to keep digging until he figures things out."

"He might, yeah. Just keep your guard up."

Easy for her to say; she wasn't faced with hanging out with him all the time. She didn't have to watch him fight or resist his kisses. I did, and it was hard to remember why I shouldn't like him.

Especially since I didn't want to live a life of secrets and lies. For once, I'd like to be honest with someone besides my *deirfiúr*. I loved them, but it wasn't the same.

"So you didn't find the scroll?"

Nix's words jerked me to attention. "No. And it's worse than that. Demons took it. The same kind of demon who called me a FireSoul the other day."

Nix abruptly stopped pacing. "What? Did they say anything else?"

"No. I tackled one and demanded that he tell me what he knew, but he just looked at me."

"There might not be a link. Just because they're the same species doesn't mean they all know about us. That other demon might have known because he was ancient and could sense it."

"Yeah, maybe," I said. "But we haven't stayed alive this long by assuming things are coincidences."

135

"True."

"There was also a man there. A Magica. But he didn't give a crap about me. Grabbed the scroll and left."

"Well that's good."

"Yeah. But we have our concealment charms, so maybe that's why."

"At least they're still working."

"They'd better be," I said. "They cost a freaking fortune. But we need to call Del. Warn her to keep her guard up. Just in case."

"I'll do it. You need to rest."

"Yeah. I think I might go talk to Dr. Garriso. He could know more about that kind of demon." There were hundreds of kinds. I didn't know them all—or even most of them. Half the time I made up names for them based on what they looked like. I called these ones shadow demons because they were gray. Not very clever.

"I can do it. You really do look like you're about to pass out."

"No, I want to. I can describe them best. I'll do it after I take a nap."

"Fine. And tomorrow you'll find the scroll and destroy it. We'll deal with your nightmare man when the time comes. We've always known we were on the run. Eventually, we'll get caught."

"Then we fight."

"If we have to, yes."

"But how do we do that without magic?"

"I don't know." Distress was thick in Nix's voice. "We've repressed most of what we have to stay safe. But if there's a bigger threat out there than the Prison for Magical Miscreants, we're screwed."

"Then you think we should practice our magic?" Practicing would mean I wouldn't feel like hell after using it, but that wouldn't do me any good if I got caught.

"I don't know. Is this scroll—and whoever is looking for us—a bigger threat than being thrown in prison?"

"We're digging into our past with this scroll. Maybe this whole thing will lead us to our parents." Hope flared in my chest, though I knew it was stupid. They were probably dead. Or they were the ones we were running from.

I hated not knowing.

"I don't want to hope for that," Nix said. "We've made a good life for ourselves here. I want to look to the future."

I nodded. Though I'd love to find my parents, I agreed. Our first five years on the run had been horrible. We'd laid low out of fear, sticking to back alleys and abandoned farms, stealing only what wouldn't be noticed. If we'd been any less afraid, we might have used our magic more and been caught.

As it was, we'd gotten ourselves tangled up in some ugly messes. But we'd made it out. We'd survived and learned about the world. Found our way to Magic's Bend and built our shop.

I had to find this scroll and destroy it. We couldn't lose the life we'd worked so hard for.

Nix rubbed my shoulder and got to her feet. "Get some rest. I'm going to call Del."

"Thanks," I said as she left.

When the door shut behind her, I flopped back onto the couch and stared at the ceiling. Sweat and dust covered my skin. It itched.

I should get up and shower.

Instead, I slowly careened over onto the couch.

Sometime later—hours or minutes, I had no idea— the sound of rain on the windows woke me. I scrubbed my eyes with the heel of my hand and squinted into the dark night. The clock by the door indicated that it was past nine.

My mouth tasted like a rodent had died in it, and I was still as gross as ever.

Excellent.

But when I stood, I felt better. Like I'd just recovered from a bad case of the flu, but at least I could walk to the shower.

Careful not to rub any of the dried blood off my daggers, I took them into the bedroom. Normally I stored them on my bedside table, but the blood on Righty was the only link to the Magica who'd stolen the scroll.

That made it the most valuable thing I owned. And valuable things belonged in the trove, hidden away from all but me.

I laid my hand on the hidden door in my bedroom. The enchantment unlocked at my touch, and I pushed the door open.

I flicked on the light, a sense of calm flowing over me as the golden light reflected off the leather and metal stacked neatly on shelves and hung from racks. It was like a library, shelves and aisles of the things I valued most. Though part of me coveted gold whenever I saw it, I thought that was more of a knee-jerk reaction, because whenever I had money to spend, the first things I looked for were leather goods and weaponry.

I walked toward the back, making my way slowly so that I could absorb as much calm as possible from my favorite place.

At the very back corner, I dropped to my knees. My least valuable boots and jackets were stored back here, but it was a facade. I pushed aside a pair of older boots and pressed my hand to the tiny, invisible door.

My touch ignited the spell and it popped open. The battered golden locket that I'd been wearing when I'd woken in that field ten years ago glinted. Once, I'd hoped it'd lead me to my parents, but I'd been wrong.

I touched it briefly, then placed the daggers inside the safe. The door shut with a soft click. I rose to my feet and headed to the shower to cram myself into the little space. Though the pipes screamed and hissed, the water was usually hot and floods were infrequent.

It didn't take long to scrub off the grime. By the time I got out, I was feeling almost human again.

Except for the fact that my stomach was trying to eat itself.

I tugged on jeans and a tank top, dreading the walk down the street to get food from P & P. I could order in from a delivery place, but that could take an hour. There was a chance I could scavenge from my kitchen, but the odds of finding something decent weren't high.

My stomach grumbled loudly, objecting.

"All right, all right," I muttered. I needed to get out anyway. Dr. Garriso worked late most nights. I could grab a bite to eat and head by his office for some info.

I was throwing on my jacket when a knock sounded at the door. My muscles tensed, and I crept silently over to it, peering out through the peep hole. Nix had a goofy knock, and Del was out of town.

Aidan.

Of course.

CHAPTER NINE

The rich scent of curry wafted through the door, so I yanked it open. What could I say? I was weak.

He held up a large white sack, a grin tugging at his handsome face. "Delivery."

Oh man, I wanted that food. But I really didn't want to let him into my house. He probably wouldn't figure out that I had a trove behind the walls, but I hated to risk it.

"Why are you here?" I asked.

"I thought you'd be hungry."

"You want to interrogate me."

"Nah. I just thought you'd be hungry." Sincerity shone in his eyes.

Butterflies set up a cacophonous racket in my stomach, which wasn't hard considering how empty it was. I glared at Aidan, knowing that I looked unwelcoming but having a hard time wrapping my head around him. Confusion pissed me off.

"What's your deal?" I asked. "I bet you live over in Enchanter's Bluff." There was no way a guy as wealthy as him didn't live in the rich section of town. "It's got to be a thirty-minute drive over here. Just to bring me food?"

"It was worth the drive."

"Why?"

"To see you."

Okay, this was so outside of my pay grade. Killing demons and stealing treasure—that was about all I was qualified for. Hot dudes trying to woo me? Not so much.

At least, I assumed this was wooing. Bringing a girl food sure sounded like wooing to me.

"This isn't a date," I said.

"No," he agreed. "Definitely not a date. You'll know when it's a date. This is just me bringing you food because I knew you'd be beat when you woke up."

I tried not to let the sentiment get to me, but it poked me in the heart all the same. Not only did I want to devour whatever was in the white takeout bag, I wanted to hang out with Aidan. Even though I knew it was a bad idea.

I weighed suggesting eating in the shop below versus letting him in. A sigh heaved out of me.

"Come on in." Letting him in was less suspicious, and he didn't need any more reasons to think I was hiding something.

"Thanks." He stepped inside, and I shifted so that he wouldn't go toward my bedroom. It meant I had to stand nearer to him, which just made my heart start to pound faster.

"Kitchen's that way." I tilted my head toward the doorway on the other side of the room and stifled a small sigh of relief when he walked toward it.

"You got any beer?" he asked as he entered the kitchen.

I followed him in, helplessly sniffing the scented air he left in his wake. "In the fridge. Help yourself."

My kitchen was tiny and almost completely nonfunctional. All the appliances were ancient. Not retro in a cool way. Just ancient. With P & P down the street, there was no reason to cook. And all my money was tied up in the trove. I was probably a hoarder, but at least it was all packed away neatly in a secret closet.

I grabbed some paper plates and plastic utensils from the cupboard.

"PBR?" Aidan asked.

I turned to see him standing in front of the fridge, holding two cans. "Yeah? Got a problem with that?"

"Never pegged you for a hipster-beer kinda girl."

"That's hillbilly beer, thank you very much," I said as I grabbed one. "And hipsters drink microbrew too, you know. I bet you drink microbrew."

He raised his hands. "So I like a decent beer every now and again."

"This is decent beer!" I held it out in front of his face. "Look, right there on the label! It says Blue Ribbon. That means it's good. Blue Ribbons are for winners."

He grinned.

He was screwing with me.

"Just bring the food," I said as I headed to the living room.

Though there was a little round table pushed in front of the window on the other side of the room, I preferred to eat on the couch whenever possible. Since I still wasn't feeling one hundred percent, I veered toward the couch.

I plopped down and put the plates on the table, then opened my icy beer and took a swig.

"So what if this doesn't have much taste," I said. "It's refreshing and delightful. PBR delivers."

Aidan gave me a skeptical look as he sat next to me and popped his can. "I'll try to re-approach it with an open mind."

I watched him drink, trying to keep my eyes off the motion of his strong throat as he swallowed.

Okay, I was clearly going nuts if I was looking at a guy's throat and getting the hots for him. But I couldn't help it. All of him was hot—from his model face to his sculpted muscles. Why couldn't he look like a normal dude? That wouldn't make my mind get all fuzzy.

When Aidan lowered his can, he caught me staring at him. I almost slumped with relief when he said, "Not too bad," instead of calling me out for staring.

"Yeah, it's pretty good, right? And cheap. There's loads to love about it."

"Don't know if I'd say *love*."

"Just get the food out, Mr. Critic."

He pulled several cartons out of the bag, along with a paper-wrapped parcel of Naan bread. I made grabby hands, and he passed me a carton that smelled like curry.

"Okay," I said as I swallowed a bite that I'd scooped up with the bread, "I'm officially thanking you for bringing this over. It's amazing."

"No problem."

We ate in companionable silence for a few minutes. Once the beast was sated, I asked, "So, you've got some healing ability and you're a full Elemental Mage. What else can you do?"

"Turn into any creature, real or mythical," he said. "You know, nothing interesting. Just griffons and dragons—that sort of thing."

"Cocky." I punched him in the shoulder. "Anything else?"

"You'll just have to get to know me better."

That wasn't going to happen. "Have you ever heard of another shifter/Magica hybrid?"

He shook his head. "I was an only child. My father was the Origin before me, and my mother was Magica. I don't know why it passed down to me, but I've never met another."

I scowled into my now-empty carton. I liked Aidan. For his sake, it was great he was powerful. Like, ridiculously powerful. But no one was throwing him in prison. Just my kind.

Self-disgust washed over me. I needed to quit moping. Just because this threat was looming over our heads didn't mean I wouldn't get us out of it. And people had an actual good reason to fear FireSouls. If we were power-hungry monsters, we'd have a good reason to go on a killing, power-collecting rampage.

"You okay?" Aidan asked.

"Yeah, just tired." A food coma was coming on. My eyelids felt like they weighed ten pounds each.

"You need to practice your magic," Aidan said. "If you did, you wouldn't be so exhausted after using it."

"Sounds like a me-problem, not a you-problem."

"It's a me-problem if you're working for me."

I scowled at him. "I'm not working for you for long, so don't worry about it."

"Then it's a problem because I like you," he added.

His words hit me right between the eyes. This was why relationships were dangerous. People worried about you and poked into your personal stuff. And my personal stuff was enough to get me locked up in hell. I needed to forget how freaking hot he was and move on.

"Uh, it's time for me to hit the hay. Thanks for bringing dinner."

"Fine. We'll table this for now, but it's not done. It's not safe for you to do your job if you can't control your powers. You're unique. You need to be able to control that."

"Let me worry about that."

"For now." He put his hand on my shoulder. "Hang on."

"Yeah?"

He didn't say anything, but his healing warmth soaked into my shoulder. I barely resisted leaning into him, but it felt so good. Once he removed his hand, I felt amazingly better. Not one hundred perfect, but definitely able to leave the house.

"I'll see you tomorrow morning at seven," he said as he got up.

"All right. Let's meet at Potions & Pastilles. I can't function at that hour without coffee." And I didn't need him coming back to my place again.

"Okay." He let himself out.

His footsteps were silent on the stairs as I walked to the window. I watched him cross the street to his car and pull away, then I tugged on my jacket. It was past ten, but there was a good chance Dr. Garriso was still at work. He preferred the night hours.

On my way out, I went to my trove and quickly chose another pair of daggers. They weren't enchanted to return to me, but they were wickedly sharp. And the shiny copper hilt looked badass.

I crept down the stairs past Nix's door and out into the street. Clouds rolled in front of the moon, casting the night in shadows. Cecelia, old faithful herself, sat at the curb looking out of place on the trendy street. Her black paint was chipped and the bumper needed some work, but she still got me where I needed to be, so I was keeping her.

The streets of Magic's Bend were quiet as I drove through town. Things were only hopping on the weekends, and usually that activity was centered around the historic district where most of the bars were. The Museum of Magical History, where Dr. Garriso worked, was only a few miles from my apartment. I pulled into the quiet parking lot.

Rain started to fall as I hurried around the side of the building. Dr. Garriso's office was on the bottom floor at the back. The boring part, he said, where the visitors didn't want to go. When I reached his little window, I tapped on it. The golden glow of his lamps gleamed through the layer of dust on the window, and I could just make out his form rising from his desk.

I ran over to the door and hopped up and down as I waited for him. The rain was coming down harder now, and I wasn't a fan.

"Come in, come in!" he said as he unlocked the museum's back door.

I stepped into the narrow linoleum hallway. "Thanks. It's really starting to come down out there."

He peered out into the night and shook his head. "Looks like I'm not going home for a while."

"Would you have anyway?"

He shrugged one skinny shoulder and let out a creaky laugh. Dr. Garriso was about seventy, with a tuft of white hair and sharp eyes. Though he'd told me once that he was from Missouri, he favored tweed coats that would do any old British professor proud. The aesthetic fit him.

He turned and shuffled down the hall to his office. "Come on, I just put the kettle on."

I followed him down the silent hall and turned into his office and couldn't help but grin as the scent of tea and books wafted over me. I loved his office. Though the hallway outside looked like any modern, boring hallway, Dr. Garriso's office was different. It was like stepping back in time—perfect for a little old man who wore tweed coats.

It was a narrow space but long enough to look large. Every wall was covered with bookshelves that were stuffed to the brim with old leather tomes. The lights were old Tiffany lamps with yellow bulbs—none of those modern white ones for Dr. Garriso. I was pretty sure he'd use candles if they'd let him.

I took a seat in one of the two wingback chairs at the far end of the office. I sank into it like it was a cloud. They were right under the window, though they looked like they should be in front of a fireplace. His desk was at the other end. In the middle, near the door, was the table with the tea supplies.

"What brings you to my office?" Dr. Garriso asked as he poured water from an electric kettle into a chipped coffee mug. He dumped in five sugar cubes and fixed a plain one for himself, then joined me.

"Thanks," I said as I took the coffee mug he held out. I sipped, then cursed.

"You know you should wait," he said as he lowered himself slowly into his chair.

"I know. But you make the best tea."

"Hummingbird food," he said.

"Yeah, yeah, so I like sugar." But I grinned. I liked being around Dr. Garriso. It didn't take a shrink to figure out that since I couldn't remember my parents, I was probably looking for some kind authority figure as a stand-in.

But whatever. Psychoanalyzing myself wasn't going to do me any good. I'd just enjoy Dr. Garriso's company and hopefully get my answers.

"I have a question about some demons that I've been encountering."

"What kind?"

"I call them shadow demons because they're gray and throw smoke when they fight. They've also got big arms and narrow horns that run back along their heads.

I've been seeing them all over the place lately. One of them knew something they shouldn't."

"Shouldn't how?"

"It's kinda a secret."

"I don't suppose you'll tell me what it is?"

"'Friad I can't." Truth was, I honestly didn't think Dr. Garriso would turn me in to the Order of the Magica. But I couldn't risk it.

"That's all right." Dr. Garriso tapped his chin and scrunched his brow. "Interesting. I think I might know just the kind of demon you're talking about."

He set his tea down and stood, then walked slowly along the bookshelves, examining the titles.

"That's it!" he muttered as he pulled down a big leather-bound one and brought it back. He sat and flipped through it, his brow creased.

"Ah! That's it," he said a few minutes later, his finger pressed to a page. He passed it to me. An illustration of one of the gray bastards stared back.

"You found them!" I said, then glanced at the heading. "Eshkanawinawel?"

"Some of them have rather long names," he said as he reached for the book. I handed it over and he skimmed it. "Their language is a complex one. I believe Eshkanawinawel means Smoke Thrower."

"I think I'll keep calling them shadow demons."

"Fair enough." Dr. Garriso skimmed the book again. "Ah, yes," he muttered. "As I thought. They look very similar to Karst Demons, Grayskin Demons, and Fallow Demons. It is the smoke throwing that is one of their primary distinguishing factors."

I felt a little better about not freaking out earlier about these demons. They hadn't thrown smoke at the monks' island, after all, so they could have been any number of demons.

"What else does it say?" I asked.

"Well, like most demons, they frequently act on behalf of whoever will get them out of their hells. Mercenaries. They're very low-level demons—not very intelligent, but very loyal. They often work in large numbers for whoever frees them and gives them reason to fight."

"I suppose that's a good quality in a minion."

"Yes. These demons are frequently used by those who cannot sway anyone rational to their cause. Bad people."

"Does every single demon in the species work for one person? The same bad person?"

Dr. Garriso glanced down at the book, his eyes darting across the page. He looked back up at me. "No. They come from a large hell. Very old. I would imagine that there are several unsavory types hiring Eshkanawinawel demons."

A tiny sigh of relief escaped me. And old hell equaled old demons. And if there were so many, it was likely that the demon who'd guarded the Chalice of Youth had nothing to do with the other demons.

I'd still stay on my guard, but there was no reason to freak out just yet.

"Does that help?" Dr. Garriso asked.

"Yes. Thank you, Dr. Garriso."

"It's no problem at all. Is there anything else I can do for you?"

I shook my head. "No, but thank you. I need to get going."

He stood and walked me out. "Good luck with whatever it is you are facing."

"Thank you." I thought I might need it.

I fell into bed when I got home. My mind raced a mile a minute even after I closed my eyes and tried to sleep, so when the dream started, I didn't even realize it was a dream. Everything was black behind my eyelids, as if I were still awake and thinking.

But the smell was different from my bedroom. Dank, like water dripping down stone. There was more stone beneath me as well. And at my back. I crouched in the corner, pressing myself against a wall, as if trying to disappear. I felt like I could drown in fear; it filled my lungs, making it hard to breathe.

Nearby, someone wept softly. Two people, I realized. I squinted into the dark, trying to see them, but all I saw was darkness. The sound of skittering feet came from behind me.

Rats. I couldn't see them, but I knew. My heart pounded, the sound thunderous in my ears. But the footsteps were louder than even my heart.

Terror streaked through me and I sobbed.

The footsteps were coming closer. Coming for me?

I squeezed myself into a ball, trying to disappear into the stone. If I could just make myself small enough, he wouldn't find me.

But if he didn't find me, he'd take the other girls instead. Protectiveness welled in me. I could jump on him. Fight him. Then we'd run.

The door crashed open and light blinded me. It pounded into my head like flame. I jerked up in bed, gasping.

Shuddering, I fumbled for the bedside light. It clicked on, glowing softly. My bedroom.

Sweat covered my skin, and my lungs heaved as I sucked in air. Felt like I'd run miles. I looked around my room. At my hands. At anything that would place me in the real world and not the dream world.

I was in my bedroom. I was okay.

I was safe in Magic's Bend. I buried my face in my hands as my shoulders shook. I wasn't back there, I wasn't back there, I wasn't back there.

I'd never had that dream before. Was that my past? Had Del and Nix and I been locked up somewhere?

CHAPTER TEN

By the time I blearily stumbled into Potions & Pastilles the next morning, I was desperate for a coffee. Though the sleep had done me good, I wouldn't be functional without some caffeine.

P & P was empty that early, thank magic. Waiting in line would have been a bitch.

"Whoa, the dead walks," Connor said as I entered. He glanced at the clock behind the counter. "Six forty-five. I don't think I've ever even seen you prior to nine."

"Har har," I said. But he was right. I'd never been a morning person. I prayed to magic that Aidan wouldn't be early. I'd dragged myself out of bed just so I could have fifteen minutes with a coffee to get my mind ready to deal with him.

"The usual?" Connor asked as he turned to the espresso machine.

"Please." I climbed onto one of the three barstools at the small counter and peered into the glass display case next to me. Connor had only put out the cinnamon buns, but they looked delicious. Icing dripped from their golden crust, and sticky cinnamon paste clung to all the nooks and crannies.

"Those look amazing," I said as Connor put my latte in front of me. His apron was covered in flour again, but as usual, his t-shirt and jeans were spotless.

"Want one?"

"Two." I was going to need all the energy I could get.

Connor pulled out the tray and put a plate of two in front of me. "So, what brings you to my esteemed establishment so early in the morning?"

"Your fine company."

He laughed. "Bull. You're meeting that dude again."

"It's for a job."

"Yeah, yeah. But he looks at you like you're more than a job. Dude likes you."

I stuffed a cinnamon bun into my face to avoid talking. Connor would just give me more shit if I protested. He'd adopted me and my *deirfiúr* as sisters and treated us like he treated Claire. Which meant, though I loved him, that he was a big pain in the butt sometimes.

"This is great," I said when I swallowed. "Is there nutmeg in these?"

His face brightened. Jackpot. Connor loved baking like I loved running through enchanted tombs. It was like an extension of his potion-making talents. This had to distract him.

"Yeah," he said. "I took a bit of nutmeg and some—"

The door creaked behind me, and I turned as Connor said, "Hey, Aidan. What can I get you?"

Aidan smiled. "Triple espresso would be great, thanks. To-go cup."

"Coming right up."

"You should try the cinnamon buns," I said.

He reached for the second one on my plate, and I pulled it away, scowling. "Not mine, you monster. Connor will get you one."

"Did you fail kindergarten?" he asked.

"Kindergarten?"

"That's where people learn to share."

"Uh, yeah." I shoved the second cinnamon bun into my mouth. Not only did I not want to talk about it, I didn't want to even think about the fact that I couldn't remember kindergarten.

"Thanks," Aidan said to Connor as my friend handed him the paper cup and a bag with a cinnamon bun.

When Aidan handed over a twenty, Connor said, "Don't worry about it. On the house."

"Don't give him stuff," I said. "He'll keep coming back if you feed him."

"That's the point. We've got to get you a man somehow," Connor said.

"You're the worst." I threw the last bite of my cinnamon bun at him, mournfully watching it fly through the air. "The actual worst. Good day to you, sir."

I hopped off the stool and faced Aidan. "Ready?"

"Yeah." He glanced back at Connor. "Thanks, man."

"Anytime, bro."

Ugh. They were buddies. This couldn't be good.

I led the way out to Aidan's car and climbed into the passenger seat. At least the day was going to be clear and bright. The sky was a brilliant blue, and the birds were singing their butts off.

"You know the way to Darklane?" I asked.

"Yeah. Whenever we have a break-in at one of the properties we secure, there's a good chance the culprit lives in Darklane."

"Lead on, then."

Aidan navigated through town while I wished I'd asked for another coffee to go. Surreptitiously, I reached for his to-go cup and took a sip.

"Gah," I spat after I'd swallowed. "Lighter fluid."

"Griffon fuel."

"I guess." I wiped my mouth. "That'll teach me to snitch your drinks."

He grinned. I glanced quickly out the window to keep myself from mooning over him. We'd entered the business district of town. There were a few tall buildings, none over ten stories.

"Do you have an office here?" I asked.

He nodded and pointed to the left, where the grandest building stood. "That one."

"I should have guessed."

The business district gave way to the historic district. These buildings had been here since the early seventeen hundreds and it showed. The architecture was like something out of the old world. European supernaturals had made it out here earlier than human settlers and established Magic's Bend in 1712. There'd been some trouble with the Native American supernaturals—which was bound to happen when you invaded someone's land—but that had been settled eventually with a peace treaty.

It wasn't like supernaturals were any more peaceful than humans—definitely not. There'd been an ugly war leading up to the peace treaty, but the result had been a stable alliance that had allowed Magic's Bend to grow into the largest magical city in America.

"Do you ever come down here?" Aidan asked as we drove through the bustling streets of the historic district.

There was a lot more foot traffic here, drawn by the shops and restaurants that made up the bottom floors of the old buildings. Though almost everyone looked human, I spotted a few fae with their wings out and one huge dude who looked like he was half giant. Though many supernaturals went out amongst humans—and even lived amongst them—non-human looking supernaturals were required by law to stay in wholly magical cities like Magic's Bend.

"I come down here occasionally," I said. "But I mostly hang out on Factory Row."

My neighborhood had been revitalized in the 1990s when the abandoned factories from the nineteenth and early twentieth centuries had been turned into apartments and shops, mostly antique places. P & P and the Flying Wizard were the only two bars on that side of town, but they worked fine for my socializing needs. It didn't have quite the same charm as the historic district, but it suited me. And it was the only place where we could afford apartments big enough to stash our hoards.

"Do you come down here a lot?" I asked as we finally passed out of the historic district and into Darklane.

"Darklane? No. Only when work brings me here," Aidan said. "But yes to the historic side of town. They've got some good restaurants. We'll have to try one when this job is over."

"We'll see." I turned my attention to the buildings that passed slowly by the car. Darklane was on the other side of the historic district, and it suited its name. The buildings were all three stories tall here, though they somehow managed to block out a lot of the sun. They were as old as the buildings we'd just left behind, but these really showed their age. Not only was the architecture ancient, but so was the layer of grime that covered the brick and wood.

Contrary to what one might think, this wasn't the poor side of town. It was where you lived if you worked with magic's darker side. The kind that harmed as well as accomplished goals. But just because it harmed didn't make it bad. It was all up to interpretation.

While a lot of these supernaturals were occasionally on the wrong side of the law, they weren't outright lawbreakers. The Magica would crack down on that. They walked the line with things like blood magic— illegal if you do it without the consent of the donor, but otherwise acceptable. Their magic cast a shadow over the buildings. It was hard not to make the comparison of dark versus light magic, though it wasn't that simple.

Aidan slowed the car to a crawl as we neared the address. We rolled by the narrow buildings. If I squinted,

I could make out the color underneath the grime. The buildings had once been brightly painted.

"There it is," I pointed to a building that had once been purple. The windows were dark, the stairs leading up to the stoop narrow and rickety. A sign hung over the door that read Apothecary's Jungle.

Aidan pulled the car over and parked in front of Mordaca's home. He moved in front of me as we climbed the creaking stairs. He was trying to block me from danger. While part of me was annoyed by it, the smart part of me thought *let him*.

A brass lion door knocker scowled at us from the dark purple door. Aidan knocked it and the lion roared. I grinned. I kinda liked Mordaca already.

But it wasn't Mordaca who answered. A hulking, shirtless man with wild golden hair pulled open the door. His scowl turned into widened eyes. He stepped back and bowed.

"Origin." His deep voice was laced with respect.

Whoa. So shifters took this Origin thing seriously. I assumed he was a shifter. His magic smelled animalistic, with a hint of something else. Something dry—like the desert. Maybe the plains of Africa? I'd never been, but I guessed that might be what I was smelling. With his crazy golden hair streaked through with hundreds of shades, I'd bet lion.

"Lion," Aidan greeted.

"I am Mathias," the lion said as he stepped back. "Welcome."

"Just who are you letting into my house at this ungodly hour?" an annoyed female voice asked from within.

Mathias stepped back, pulling the door farther open. Though the foyer was dim, I could make out the stairs leading upward. The woman who descended looked like Elvira's cousin. No joke. Bouffant black hair, a slinky, plunging dress of the same shade, and so much eye makeup she looked like she was wearing a Zoro mask.

It was only seven thirty, and she was more put together than I ever was. Her magic rolled over me in waves. She was strong. Not nearly as strong as Aidan, but very powerful. Her magic prickled at my skin—kind of like rolling a hairbrush over my arm. The only other sense I got off of her was the taste of whiskey. I never understood why people's magic tasted the way it did, but I assumed it meant that her magic burned going down.

"This is the Origin," Mathias said.

"My friend Claire called about us yesterday," I said. "We need help with a tracking spell."

"Oh, yes. I remember," Mordaca said. "We've just returned from LA, and I was about to head to bed."

So this was evening for her. That explained why she was so done up at such an early hour when she really didn't look like a morning person. In my head, morning people were always wearing workout clothes and perky smiles. The only thing perky about Mordaca was her tits.

"Come in," she said, gesturing with a hand that looked like it was tipped with black claws. They were just nails filed to a point, but the effect did the trick. She looked exactly like I'd expect a Blood Sorceress to look.

This was the chick that Connor had the hots for? Wow, kid.

I followed Aidan into the dark foyer, trying not to wrinkle my nose at the overpowering incense that wafted from a back room.

"You can go upstairs, pet." Mordaca patted the lion's bare chest and he growled, but he did as she said. "Come with me."

We followed her to the door at the back of the foyer. The black and white tiled floor and the ornately carved ceiling were cleaner than I'd expected. The dark and the smell made me think there'd be a thick layer of cobwebs, but I could see none.

The foyer led to a cluttered back room. Shelves of jars and crystals covered the walls, and a big wooden table stood in the middle. A workshop. A hearth burned in the corner, and herbs hung from the ceiling.

"Do you sell a lot of charms?" I asked.

Mordaca rounded the table to stand across from us. "Not many. They're difficult to make, and not many people are willing to pay what I ask." Her gaze met Aidan's. "But the Origin will have no problem with that."

Aidan nodded as I looked around covetously. I itched to explore the shelves and see what magic bits and bobs she had lying around. Because I didn't use my own power, I relied heavily on charms like my comms necklace and my daggers. But like Mordaca had said, enchanting objects was difficult, so there weren't many lying around, and they were damned pricey when you could get your hands on them. Magic had a hard time surviving away from its master. It was one of the reasons my business dealing in ancient enchanted artifacts did so well.

If I were willing to use my magic, I could borrow Mordaca's power and enchant my own objects. But that wasn't worth the risk.

"What can I do for you?" Mordaca asked.

Carefully, I drew Righty from its sheath and held it out. I'd wrapped the blade in plastic wrap to protect the blood, and it glinted in the low light. "There's blood on this blade. I want to track whoever it belongs to."

Mordaca reached out with her black claws and took the blade. She wrinkled her nose as she unwrapped the plastic. "Shifter, Magica, or human?"

"Magica. But I don't know what kind."

"All right." She laid it gently on the wooden table. "I'm going to need to get my sister to help me with this. It will cost more. Wait here one moment."

She left through a side door, and I glanced at Aidan. "Creepy in here, huh?"

"Not my preferred brand of magic, no," he said.

Footsteps sounded a moment later. Another woman followed Mordaca into the room. Though she looked like Mordaca, she was pale where her sister was dark. She wore a white robe that covered her to her neck, and she yawned as she took up a spot next to Mordaca.

"I am Aerdeca." Her voice was sweeter, without the raspy undertones that Mordaca's voice carried, but it resonated with power all the same. I couldn't taste her magic like I could with Mordaca, but the sound of chirping birds accompanied her, along with the feeling of a light breeze. She practiced blood magic like her sister, but I couldn't pinpoint why she felt so different. Like a white witch to Mordaca's dark witch.

Two sides of a coin?

"Morning," I said once I realized I'd been feeling out her magic for too long. I needed to not do that. People got weird when you stared at them for so long.

"Yes, early isn't it?" She looked like she liked mornings as much as I did. She must have kept a schedule that was the opposite of Mordaca's. This wasn't her evening—it was her coffee hour, and we were interrupting.

Mordaca looked at me. "I am going to need some things from you to enhance the spell."

Suspicion loomed. "What kind of things?"

"You really want to find him, right? That desire will help fuel the spell. So a drop of your blood." She turned to Aidan. "From you as well."

No surprise. She wasn't called a Blood Sorceress for nothing.

When she gestured with her claws, I held out my hand. She nicked my finger with a small silver blade, and I let my blood drip into the small bowl she held out. At least she didn't use her claw. When she let go of my hand, I stuck my cut finger into my mouth.

"Now you." She held out her hand to Aidan. Once they'd completed the task, she looked back at me. "The addition of something that you value will enhance the spell."

"That I value? Like what?" But my eyes darted to my blade. That was pretty damned valuable to me.

Her gaze followed mine. "This blade?"

"I value it, but I really don't want to give it up. It's part of a pair."

"That's the point. The spell might work without it, but sacrifice gives it juice."

"What about Aidan?" I asked.

"Him as well," she said.

"I don't have anything with me that I really value," he said.

I eyed the fancy watch at his wrist, but for a guy like him, that probably wasn't anything special.

Mordaca's gaze searched him, then landed on me. "No. There is only one thing you value in this room, and I don't think I can put her into the spell. That just leaves the dagger."

Uh, hello, what? He valued me? I had no idea how to respond to that, so I just said, "Fine."

I had brought my copper-hilt daggers as backup, but I hated to give up the obsidian. It was my fave.

Mordaca nodded and picked up the glass blade. She held it point down over the bowl, and her hand began to glow. Slowly, the dagger lit from within—a bright purple that burned my eyes. I squinted as the blood on the blade turned black, then dripped off into the bowl. It sizzled, letting off an acrid smoke. The taste of whiskey at the back of my throat grew. I wondered if Aidan got the same sense of Mordaca's power.

A second later, my obsidian blade turned to liquid as well, dripping into the bowl. My heart ached at the sight. That dagger had kept me safe for a long time.

Mordaca stirred the contents with one black fingernail, then handed the bowl to Aerdeca. The blonde sorceress lifted it in front of her chest and circled her hand over the bowl. A white light glowed from her palm, extending out to envelop the bowl. The air hummed with her magic, and the wind that accompanied it picked up. It didn't look like my clothes were blowing in it, but it felt like it.

The dark liquid in the bowl began to spin, rising up like a little tornado until it formed a ball. When the ball turned from black to clear, Aerdeca snatched it out of the air and put the bowl on the table.

"All done." Aerdeca handed it to her sister.

"Nicely done," Mordaca said.

"Nice to meet you." Aerdeca turned to leave. The words didn't sound sincere. "Next time, don't come so early."

That had sounded sincere, however.

She left the room, taking with her the sound of birds and the feeling of a breeze.

Mordaca held out the little glass ball. "This will lead you to your prey."

I reached out for it, and she snatched it back.

"For a price."

Oh, damn. We hadn't talked price. I hadn't even realized. "You're waiting until after to tell us the price?"

"Once you see what you've requested, you want it more." She rolled the glass ball in her palm. "So you'll pay more. I'm a businesswoman."

So was I, and I knew that we weren't above gouging people who could afford it. "How much?"

"A favor. From you."

"Not from the big guy?" I nodded at Aidan.

"No. He's powerful, but you're good at finding things."

"So are you." I really didn't want to owe her one. She was dangerous.

"It's something I can't find. Just like this charm"— she held up the glass ball—"is for something that you can't find. We all have our blind spots."

"What is it?"

"I prefer not to say until you agree."

Okay, that definitely made my spidey sense pop up. "Sorry, no can do."

"She's right," Aidan said. "I'm the one seeking this Magica, not her. I'll pay."

Mordaca huffed her disappointment, then turned her sharp gaze on Aidan. "Fine. Twenty grand."

I almost choked on my gasp.

"Will you take a card?" Aidan asked. "I believe I'm a bit short on cash."

No joke.

"Of course. What kind of operation do you think this is?"

I glanced at the herbs and crystals and incense. A creepy one! She was a freaking Blood Sorceress, for magic's sake!

"Excellent." Aidan handed over his card, and she pulled a phone out of her dress pocket. It had one of those little swipey things on it, and within a minute she'd taken his payment and handed over the glass ball.

She looked at me. "You'll use that glass ball to find the link to the Magica you seek. It will jumpstart your own tracking ability. Just hold it close and do what you normally would when you are seeking."

"Sounds easy enough."

"It should be. Good doing business with you. Please come back soon." She waved—more of a finger wiggle than anything else.

"We're dismissed," I muttered to Aidan.

"Exactly," Mordaca said. "I need my beauty sleep."

"Thanks for your help," Aidan said.

I followed him out of the room and through the dim foyer. We let ourselves out onto the bright street. The sunlight just made this part of Darklane look even dingier.

"That wasn't so bad," I said as we walked to his car.

"Speak for yourself. I just paid for a midsize car, and all I got was this glass ball."

"Worth it, though." Even if I'd had to come up with the cash, I'd have found a way. We really needed to get that scroll.

"Very much so."

We climbed into his car. I reached out for the ball. "Let's do this thing. I want to know where those bastards are."

Aidan handed it over. The ball was cool and heavy in my hand. I held it close to my chest and focused on my memory of the man who'd stolen the scroll. Mordaca's magic twined with mine. Hers smelled musky and felt dark. Though it made my skin prickle, it didn't feel evil like some people's magic. It smelled like cigar smoke and tasted like whiskey.

After a moment, the familiar string wrapped around my waist, pulling me. Our prey was close. A sense of the location bloomed within me, clear as glass.

I sucked in a breath.

"They're at Ancient Magic," I gasped.

CHAPTER ELEVEN

The drive to Ancient Magic felt like it took forever. Aidan drove like a demon, breaking at least five traffic laws. By the time he pulled up beside my shop, I was vibrating with tension.

The car screeched to a halt at the curb. I flung the door open and leapt out. Ancient Magic's door was shattered, jagged pieces of glass protruding like teeth. Within, figures fought, wrestling on the ground and throwing magic in bursts of smoke.

Shadow demons. An icicle of fear pierced my heart, sending cold streaking through me. They had found us.

I drew my copper-hilt knives and burst into the shop.

There were at least five demons fighting Nix, Claire, and Connor. Even Del was there, wielding her short sword like a master against the same man from the tomb in Norway. He was the only non-demon assailant, but he was strong. He threw blasts of flame at Del that she repelled with her enchanted sword. Blade and shield in one, it was her first choice of weapon.

How had he found us? Fear sunk its claws into my back. My magic surged within me, a tidal wave of power that threatened to overwhelm my control and burst out of me in a horrifying show of force. I could blast them all away, but I couldn't keep my magic from hurting my *deirfiúr* as well. Or Connor and Claire, who fought two huge demons in the back corner.

Nix grappled with two in front of the counter. Behind her, a demon ransacked the shelves. In quick succession, I threw both of my copper-hilt daggers. They plunged into his back, near where I hoped his heart would be.

The demon turned and growled. Damn. Despite the blades in his back, he was still standing. He was at least as strong as the demon at the temple of Murreagh. Not all shadow demons seemed to be that strong, but perhaps he was old.

He raised a huge gray hand and threw a blast of smoky magic at me. I dove left as the searing streak of smoke plowed into the window behind me. It shattered, throwing glass everywhere. Pain pierced my back in a hundred little places.

Damn! I climbed to my feet, my back burning, as Aidan launched himself past me at the demon who'd attacked me. He was in his human form because the shop was too small for him to fight as a griffon, but he was fierce. His fists were a blur, which was lucky, because his brand of magic was so destructive that he'd have to fight with fists if he didn't want to destroy the building he was in.

I leapt over debris in the middle of the shop, my heart aching at the sight of all the broken replicas, and joined Nix in fighting the two demons that attacked her. She'd been fine when I'd first burst into the store, fighting the demons off with her usual skill, but one had gotten in a solid hit to her middle that had her wheezing.

We each took one demon—like a double date, but way more violent. The punch I threw at my demon glanced off his face. My knuckles burned. This was why I hated hand-to-hand.

I ducked down and grabbed a jagged piece of shattered pottery. It was shaped roughly like a dagger, and I plunged it into the demon's chest and then kneed him between the legs, hoping I was getting a ball shot. As he collapsed, I caught sight of Aidan charging the man who'd fought Del.

She was sprawled on the ground, her dark hair spread out in a crimson wave. The attacking Magica flung out his hand and sent a jet of ice at Aidan. The jagged blue wave of ice plowed him to the ground.

Oh, man, I wished I could use my power to blast him back. The bastard so deserved it. None of us wanted to destroy Ancient Magic, so we didn't use our powers. But this guy didn't care.

The man jumped over the counter. I ran for him. Before I got there, he reached under the counter and grabbed a box, then threw something to the ground. A silvery cloud burst up around him and he disappeared.

I stumbled to a halt.

What the hell? I thought he'd been after us. I spun around to check my *deirfiúr*. The demon that Nix had fought was on the ground. She knelt over Del.

Aidan slipped up behind the demon who'd fought Claire and broke its neck. It was the last demon in the shop. The rest were unconscious or had already disappeared.

"Check to see if they're all dead," I said. "I want to know why they were here."

"Robbery," Nix said. "The first real one we've had in a while."

She was right—we didn't often get thieves she couldn't take care of. But these weren't ordinary thieves. There was a lot more at play here that I didn't understand.

I knelt over the demon that Nix had knocked out and shook him. Nothing. He was just dead weight. Literally. He wasn't breathing.

He'd disappear soon, back to his hell.

"I killed this one," Aidan said. "Sorry about that."

"Mine's dead too," Connor said.

"Damn." With the promise of information gone, I sank to my knees. The pain of my wounds finally hit me. My back hurt like hell.

"Are you all right?" Aidan knelt beside me, gently touching my shoulder with one big hand.

"Yeah." I bit out the words. "Just a flesh wound."

"Not funny," he said. "How wounded are you?"

"Not as wounded as Del." I jerked my chin toward my *deirfiúr*, who still lay on the ground. "Help her."

I tried to catch my breath as Aidan knelt over Del and laid his hands on her middle. Her clothes were singed from the flame, but at least I didn't smell burning flesh. Nix looked on expectantly. She held one hand over a gash on her arm, slowing the blood flow. Connor and Claire sat with their backs against the counter, panting. Claire looked rough—her clothes were torn and her lip was bleeding. Connor looked a bit better, but not much. He was almost as good a fighter as his sister, despite his lack of practice. A natural.

Ancient Magic was a mess. Shelves were broken, replicas shattered all around us. Pottery and glass glinted on the floor, and silver and fake gold were crushed. In most cases, if the vessels containing the magic broke into too many pieces, the magic dissipated into the air, gone forever.

How much had we lost today? And why the hell had it happened? We needed to go after whoever'd done this, but not until Del was better and we'd all talked.

"How's she doing?" I leaned over Del.

"Okay." Del's voice was scratchy and her eyes weren't open yet, but there was a bit of color to her cheeks. She was dressed in her usual mercenary gear. Whereas I favored jeans and leather jackets, she was an all-leather kind of girl. It looked pretty badass with her black hair.

"She'll be fine," Aidan said. "I don't know what that guy hit her with, but it was strong."

"Felt like a rhino hit me in the gut," Del muttered. She opened her eyes and her gaze met mine. "Did he get away?"

"Yeah," I said. There was a hell of a lot more I wanted to say to her and Nix, but I couldn't. Not until I got Connor and Claire and Aidan to go away.

Del pushed herself up until she sat upright. Or at least, as upright as she could. We were all a mess. Only Aidan looked uninjured, and that was probably because he was a man who could fight like a bull.

"What happened?" I asked.

"That guy and his minions blasted through the glass door," Nix said. "There was a flash of light when it happened. It blinded me, but I'd seen how many there were right before it happened."

"They were trying to incapacitate you and not even have to fight," I said.

"Probably. Little did they know," Nix said. "I used my charm and called Del."

"I had enough power that I could come," Del said.

"Thank magic," I said.

Del could transport from anywhere in the world in a second, but she had to have enough power stored up to do so. Her power regenerated weirdly, but it wasn't a matter of practice like mine was. If I used my magic, I became so exhausted I couldn't do much for a while. I just wanted to sleep. She was physically fine after using her magic—she just didn't have any more juice for a while. It was one of the reasons she couldn't often make transport charms. It was also one of the reasons that we didn't call her home unless we really needed her.

"Shit! That reminds me," I said. "Check the demons' pockets for transport charms. They sometimes have them." Raiding demon corpses was one of my favorite tricks of the trade.

Wincing at the pain in my back, I crawled over to the demon that Nix had felled and searched his pockets. Nothing. I turned back to my friends.

"Mine already disappeared," Claire said.

"No charms in this guy's pockets," Aidan said.

"Damn. Worth a shot, anyway." I sat back down by Del. I tried not to shift my back too much. "So you made it here."

"Yeah," Del said. "Claire and Connor were already here."

"We heard the blast that took out the door," Connor said.

Guilt tugged at me. "Thanks for coming, guys. You didn't have to."

"Sure we did," Claire said. "You're our friends."

"Yeah, but our business is dangerous. Connor, at least, chose a profession that wasn't deadly. We shouldn't drag you into our mess."

Connor shrugged. "No problem. And my sis here gets antsy if she doesn't kill something every week, so this was good exercise for her."

"True," Claire said. "But what did that guy take?"

"A box. I couldn't make it out though." I gingerly climbed to my feet. As I made my way to the counter, I remembered the Chalice of Youth that Nix had stashed under there. The original.

When I looked down at the empty shelf, it was gone. Damn. I glanced at the back shelf. The replica was gone too. He must have grabbed it right before he disappeared.

What the hell?

"Thanks for your help, guys," I said to Connor and Claire. I didn't want to drag them farther into this. "You've got to be beat. Why don't you get cleaned up, and we'll meet you over at your place. No need to hang around this dump with us."

"We'll help you clean up," Connor said.

I looked around, my heart breaking at the devastation inside our shop. Half the shelves and possibly as much inventory were smashed. "I think we're going to save that for another day."

"Yeah," Nix said. "I don't think I can face that right now."

"Same," Del said.

"All right," Claire said. "We'll head over to P & P and get cleaned up. Come on by for food later."

"Thanks." I smiled at my friends as they limped out.

I glanced at Aidan. I wanted to ask him to leave so that I could speak freely with Nix and Del, but he'd never do it. Not until we'd at least discussed some of what had happened here.

"Who was that guy?" Nix asked.

"The guy from the temple in Norway," Aidan said. "He's got the scroll."

"What kind of Magica was he, Del?" I asked.

"I don't know. He threw a lot at me. Fire—he's got at least one elemental gift. But he was also hitting my mind with horrible memories. So he's got some telepathy too."

"So a mystery mage wants the scroll and the Chalice of Youth," I said. "But he grabbed the original too."

"Do you think he realized?" Del asked.

"I guess so, but I don't know how." I turned to Aidan. "Do you have any idea why that guy would want the Chalice of Youth and the scroll?"

"No. They're unrelated, as far as I know."

"Damn. I don't get it. We need to go find him."

"You need to heal, first," he said.

"I will. But could you go get us some plywood or something to cover up the door?"

Aidan looked at me suspiciously, like he knew I was trying to get him out of here for a minute.

"Please? I can't leave until the shop is at least closed up. We need something to put over the door. And we need to hire someone to enchant it." I wished I could put security enchantments on things, but I couldn't. Then I remembered what Aidan did for a living. "You're the perfect guy for it. Don't you have someone on your payroll who can come over and enchant it?"

He gave me one long look that said he wasn't going to let this go. "Yeah, I'll make a call. Then we'll deal with your back."

"My *deirfiúr* will help." My chest felt tight as I watched him rise gracefully and walk out of the shop.

"What the hell is going on?" Nix hissed as soon as he was gone. "Weren't those the shadow demons you mentioned before?"

"Yeah. I have no idea what's going on. Dr. Garriso said there are thousands of them. They can't all work for the same guy. After I talked to him, I decided it was coincidence. The demon who guarded the chalice was separate from the ones who were trying to steal the scroll. But now that they came for the chalice, it's clearly no coincidence."

"So we hunt them down," Del said. She gripped her sword.

"Yeah," I said. "We hunt them down."

"We'll go with you."

I nodded. Though part of me wanted them to stay here where it was safe, I knew they'd laugh in my face if I suggested it. Just like I'd laugh in theirs if they suggested I stay behind the front line.

"Let's get cleaned up. When Aidan gets back, we'll close up shop and follow them. The tracking charm should still work." In my panic, I'd left it in Aidan's car. I hoped he'd make sure it was all right.

Aidan walked in the door a second later.

"That didn't take you long," I said.

"I wasn't going to the hardware store for plywood."

"No?"

"No. I just made a call. It'll be here soon."

"Oh, right." He was filthy rich. Of course he didn't go to the hardware store himself. And if he did, it wasn't in moments like this, when he'd rather be interrogating me or hunting down our prey. "We're going to get cleaned up. Then we can go after that guy."

"All right. Let me help you with your back," Aidan said.

"Nix or Del will do it."

"I'm way too beat," Del said.

"Same," Nix said. "I need a shower."

I glared at them. Seriously? They were doing this because they wanted to force me and Aidan together. "Monsters", I mouthed at them.

They both shrugged, then helped each other to their feet. Del looked particularly wobbly. No surprise, considering the strength of the mystery mage.

My back burned as I stood. Every movement wiggled the glass lodged in my skin. My jacket had kept a lot of it out, but there were still some good-sized shards in there. Even the little ones burned.

A van pulled up outside the broken door. A logo on the side said Origin Enterprises, and two men in blue polo shirts hopped out. They nodded at Aidan and went to the back of the van.

As they pulled out big pieces of plywood, I asked Aidan, "Can these guys watch the shop while we get our wounds taken care of? We'll only be ten minutes, then we need to go after the thief."

"Yeah."

"Then let's do this upstairs." I'd have to take my shirt off, and I really didn't want to do it in the middle of the shop.

Aidan spoke to the repair guys while I retrieved my copper-hilt daggers and headed out the door, Nix and Del behind me. He caught up to us as we were letting ourselves in the door that led to our apartments.

We climbed silently up the stairs, Del and Nix veering off to go into Del's apartment. Aidan followed me up the next two flights to my place. I let myself in and headed straight to the bathroom.

"Give me a second alone," I said. Then I shut the door in his face.

I tried not to make any noise while I peeled my jacket off, but I really wanted to curse a blue streak. The leather pulled some of the glass out of my skin, and it tinkled when it hit the tile. I couldn't tell, but it felt like more was lodged in my t-shirt.

It took me a minute to find some scissors in the cabinet—I preferred to cut my own hair because I hated the small talk in the chair—and I cut my shirt off. It was toast anyway, and just the idea of peeling it over my head sent a streak of pain through my back. No way was I trying it in real life.

"Are you all right?"

I jumped at the sound of Aidan's voice.

"Fine!" I stifled a curse as I gingerly removed the shirt. Even more glass fell to the floor. I was sweating as I turned my back toward the mirror and peered over my shoulder.

Blood streaked everywhere and glass glinted in the light. A sigh heaved out of me. Okay, so I wasn't going to be able to take care of this myself. Hopes officially dashed.

I faced my back to the door and crossed my arms over my chest, then called, "Okay, you can come in."

Aidan's footsteps crunched on the glass as he stepped in. "Holy hell, that's bad."

"Yeah. Can you do something about it?"

"Yeah." His fresh forest scent washed over me as he stepped close.

Suddenly, my back hurt a lot less. I was more focused on how close he stood than on the glass lodged in my skin. When he laid his big hand on my shoulder, I thought I stopped breathing. His palm was warm and a bit rough, as if he worked with his hands.

Warmth radiated out from where he touched me. Sharp little pricks of pain shot from the shards of glass as my skin pushed them out. They plinked when they hit the floor.

"Most were shallow because of your jacket," Aidan said.

I'd known those jackets were a good idea.

"A few of the deeper ones will take another day to heal fully, but they shouldn't give you much problem."

"Good," I said.

"You know, you'd get hurt a lot less if you practiced and used your powers."

"I said I didn't want to talk about it."

"We don't have to talk about your parents or your past, but this is important."

My parents and past? "How do you know I have a past?"

He pulled me around so I faced him. I covered my bra with my arm. Fortunately my tits were small enough that this did some good, but I still felt exposed. His nearness made me jerk back, but he held me firm. Was I ever going to get used to how he loomed over me? His freaking shoulders were twice as wide as me.

"Everyone has a past." His voice was soft. "Most supernaturals have at least one miserable thing in it they'd like to forget. Someone with power that feels like yours probably has a really interesting past. Or a tough one."

"Powers that feel like mine?"

"Yes. Different. Stronger. There's something odd about your magic."

"I'm not odd. I'm totally normal."

"You're far from normal, but in a good way."

"Well, focus on that then instead of my weird powers. I don't use them, so it doesn't matter." I knew I was speaking too quickly, but I couldn't help it.

"It matters to me. They could protect you."

"I can protect me."

"Magic would be better. Let me help train you."

"I already told you, I blow things up. Even you can't keep me from blowing things up."

"No, but I have a lot of land. It's private. You can practice there. No one will know your powers are so uncontrollable. Temporarily uncontrollable."

"I don't know. That sounds risky." Though I really liked the idea of it. Being able to moderate the amount of power I used would be amazing. I could start to use my magic on the occasional job. More importantly, if the terrifying man from my dream ever showed up in my life again, I'd be able to fight back.

"I'll keep your secrets." Aidan's voice was rough as he lowered his head toward mine. His evergreen scent enveloped me, and I swore I could feel the warmth of him. "Whatever they are."

"I don't have any secrets," I whispered, my gaze caught on his mouth. He had the best lips. I could just stand on my tiptoes and press mine against them.

"'Course you do. All supernaturals have secrets. Like I said, I'd keep yours." He bent down farther as if he really might kiss me.

Sense snapped back into me. I was about to kiss him while talking about secrets? My secrets could kill not only me, but my *deirfiúr* as well. It hit me exactly what was at stake here. My family. Even my friends. I didn't know how much those demons knew about my past or what it all meant, but they threatened everything I loved. Aidan knowing about my past threatened everything I loved. And it might be a threat to him as well. He'd be required to report us or face punishment himself. And we really needed to get a move on with finding the guy who'd stolen the cup.

I ducked away from him and slipped out of the bathroom.

"Thanks for healing my back," I said as I ran into the bedroom. "I'll meet you downstairs in a sec."

CHAPTER TWELVE

As soon as I shut the door to my room, I remembered that I was filthy. Aidan might have gotten rid of the glass and closed the worst of my cuts, but I was still covered in blood and sweat. It itched like mad. Impatiently, I waited at my bedroom door, listening for him to leave.

When the apartment door finally opened and closed, I slipped out and went to the bathroom.

The floor was clean. He'd gotten rid of all the glass.

Hmm. He might be a threat to my safety, but cleaning the glass off my bathroom floor was pretty cool.

Ugh. I really needed to stop thinking about why he was cool. I raced through a quick shower, then threw on clothes. When it came time to put on my daggers, my shoulders slumped. My obsidian set was gone.

Damn. I'd really liked that pair.

I grabbed the copper-hilt daggers that I'd been using. After strapping on the dagger sheaths, I tugged on boots and grabbed a jacket, then ran out the door. I took the stairs two at a time, knocking on Nix's door and then Del's. They came out onto their landings by the time I was at the bottom.

"Ready?" I called.

"Yeah," said Nix. "Meet you on the street."

I went out. The morning had turned dark and dreary as rain clouds rolled over the sun. That seemed about right, since things were definitely taking a darker turn.

Aidan stood in front of my shop, talking on the phone. He nodded once, then hung up a second later. The repair guys had finished putting up the plywood and were enchanting the entire front of the shop. Blue light glowed from their hands as they ran them over the edges of the plywood.

"This holds up against pretty much any incursion," Aidan said. "You or your friends will be the only ones who can enter."

"Thanks," I said.

Footsteps sounded behind me, and I turned to see Del and Nix coming.

When they reached us, Del stuck her hand out at Aidan. "I'm Del. Didn't get a chance to introduce myself. Thanks for healing me."

Aidan took her hand. "No problem."

"We're coming with you to find the thief," Nix said.

"We can take care of it," Aidan said.

"It's personal now," Del said. "We don't take kindly to people stealing from our shop."

"Fair enough." Aidan reached into his pocket and pulled out the glass ball. He handed it to me.

"Thanks." I might not need it anymore since the Magica we sought now had the Chalice of Youth, which I'd been able to find once before, but I'd take any help I could get.

I held the ball close to my chest. Mordaca's magic seethed within the glass, reaching out and twining with mine. The scent of cigar smoke and the taste of whiskey flooded my senses, but the dark feel of her magic didn't make me nervous anymore. The tracking charm had worked once before, and I knew her magic wasn't actually evil.

I envisioned the Magica I was searching for, adding the chalice for good measure, and waited for the familiar thread to wrap around my waist and pull me.

Instead, I got a general sense of the world map, with emphasis on Scotland. Damn, he'd gone so far.

I lowered the glass ball. "He's on the west coast of Scotland. Near the Isle of Skye. Once we get there, I can get a better read on him." I looked hopefully at Del. "Do you have enough juice to transport us?"

She frowned and shook her head. "Sorry. The trip from Nicaragua was a long one. I'm burned out for at least a day, possibly two."

"It's fine," Aidan said. "I ordered that the jet be returned to Magic's Bend last night. It should be fueled by now. I'll call."

Del looked at me and mouthed, "He has a jet?"

I just shrugged. It was ridiculous that he owned a jet. Who really needed their own jet? But honestly, it was coming in really handy. Any delay in retrieving the scroll was bad, but I'd accepted that if someone had read the scroll, we'd have to kill them.

"We can take my car," Aidan said as he dialed his phone.

The four of us climbed in as Aidan ordered that the plane be prepared for flight, then we set off toward the airport. There was heavier traffic today, but Aidan weaved in and out like a pro. Or a madman. Either way, I didn't care as long as it got us to the scroll quickly.

The plane was waiting for us on the runway. A man stood at the stairs leading to the plane. He handed Aidan a duffle bag and a package.

"What's all that?" I asked as I preceded Aidan up the stairs.

"Change of clothes."

"What, you don't keep your plane stocked?"

"No, but that's a good idea."

"Your life is so different from mine," I muttered as I found a seat near a window. For the second time this week, I was boarding a private jet. I didn't need to get used to it or its cloud-like seats.

Del and Nix sat across the aisle from me.

"This is nuts," Del leaned over and whispered. "I go away for one job and you're hooking up with a guy who has his own plane."

"Shhh," I hissed back. Aidan had gone up to talk to the pilot, but I was still nervous about him overhearing. "We're not hooking up. He hired me for a job."

"Yeah, well, I could cut the tension with a knife," she said. "There's definitely something between you."

"Yeah, like the scroll we're after," I whispered. "You remember that, right? Kinda dangerous to our health?"

Her gaze sobered. "Yeah. Yeah, I do. Things have just been so good lately. We've had five good years with the shop. I guess I just thought we could hide forever."

"Me too," I said. "And we're going to. We'll handle this. Things will go back to normal."

Which reminded me that I needed to talk to them about what would happen once we found it. I glanced at the door. Still shut. I undid my seatbelt and went to kneel in front of their seats.

"What's up?" Nix whispered.

They both leaned toward me.

"How long will it take you to replicate the scroll?" I asked Nix.

She blew out a breath. "Depends. If I have to take out information about us, then I'd at least need to skim it to find the info I've got to omit."

"Damn. That'll take a while," I said. "We can't distract Aidan for that long."

"We have to destroy it," said Del. "We'll make it look like an accident."

I nodded. I hated to demolish a piece of history like that, but it was a no-brainer considering our lives were at risk. "Yeah. Okay. When we get the scroll, whoever is closest to it destroys it. The other two try to distract Aidan."

My chest ached at the idea of him finding out we'd destroyed the scroll. That would be hard to explain. We'd just have to be smart about it.

"It's a plan. We'll just—"

The cockpit door opened and Aidan stepped out. Nix shut her mouth abruptly. I stiffened, hoping we didn't look too suspicious, then turned to face Aidan.

He gave me a look that clearly asked why I was crouched on the ground instead of comfortably in my seat. I just shrugged.

Fortunately, he only said, "We'll arrive in Scotland in ten hours. I have a contact there who can have a boat ready in case we need it."

Ten hours. That'd put us there midmorning, their time.

Aidan took the seat next to mine, and I realized that Nix and Del had consciously left it open. I glared at them. They shrugged.

I should have been used to how good Aidan smelled by then, but I wasn't. I wasn't used to anything about him. I'd never been like this over a guy, and it was starting to drive me nuts.

As it turned out, we needed the boat that Aidan had arranged. The flight had been uneventful and the drive through the mountains equally so. By the time we landed, we were close enough to our prey that I finally felt the invisible string around my waist. We followed it to the coast.

My dragon sense led us to a jagged piece of land that jutted out into the sea.

"Here," I said.

Aidan pulled over. I climbed out of the car and gazed out at the choppy gray waves. Nix and Del came to stand at my side.

"Excellent," I muttered. "Another boat ride."

"Can you tell if he's on an island or a boat?"

"I don't feel the target moving," I said. But that didn't mean he wasn't. My senses weren't quite that good normally. "So it's probably an island. Could be wrong though."

Aidan looked up from the map on his phone. "There's a port about fifteen minutes from here, and the boat that I arranged isn't far from that. I'll have them meet us."

"Nice," Del said. "I could really get used to traveling with this guy."

I glanced at Aidan. He'd changed into a midnight blue sweater, and the wind whipped at his dark hair. His wealth did make things more convenient. I wished I liked him because of it. If I only liked his money, I could just ditch him and go find another rich guy who wasn't powerful enough to sense that I was different.

But no. I liked him for a lot of other weird reasons. And every one of them didn't matter because I'd definitely have to stay away from him when this was over. Aidan would eventually figure out what I was. I could feel it.

"Let's go," I said.

We climbed back into the car. The drive to the port took about fifteen minutes. It was a tiny one, just a fishing village on the coast with a few houses scattered on the hill above. Half a dozen brightly painted boats bobbed on their moorings. A large white yacht was motoring toward the small dock as we climbed out of the car.

"Is that it?" I asked Aidan.

"Yeah. A friend's boat."

"You have fancy friends."

"Some. At least this one loaned me his boat."

"You loan him your plane?" I asked.

"I would, but he has his own."

I shook my head. I might have a trove of treasure stashed away in my secret closet, but that was just because I scrimped and saved everything we made from the shop. It wasn't a tiny amount of money because treasure hunting paid well. But it wasn't like my wealth improved my life. It just fed a compulsion that was almost as annoying as it was pleasurable.

We walked onto the dock as the cold sea air cut through my jacket. Aidan carried the brown paper package. A thank you present for the boat's owner? How did he manage to be so polite while we were on a job? I guess I had to give him credit.

The boat didn't even tie off to the dock. It just pulled up and we hopped on. There was a rowboat hanging from davits at the back and a pilothouse on the second level in the front. The deckhand who led us to the pilothouse was some kind of low-level water witch from the smell of his magic. Vaguely fishy. Higher-level supernaturals normally smelled better. It was an unfair part of magical life.

The pilothouse looked like it ran a spaceship. The captain was a big guy, a shifter of some sort. I couldn't tell from the smell of him because it was harder for me to ID shifters, but I hoped he was some kind of shark or whale or something.

"Welcome aboard, Aidan," the captain said. His Scottish brogue was thick. "Mr. Carridy sends his respects."

So the owner wasn't on board.

"Captain Alden. Thank you for taking us," Aidan said. "Cass? Can you point us in the right direction?"

I focused on the feel of the string around my waist and turned to face the direction from which it pulled.

"That way," I said, pointing to the left. Port, I thought it was called. "I don't know how far. A few miles?"

"Are ye certain?" Captain Alden asked. "I've run these waters for twenty years. There's nothing that way. Not until the North Pole."

"Of course there isn't," I muttered. "Just my luck. Ghost island."

"I suppose it's possible," Captain Alden said. "Wouldn't be the first time magic has been used to hide an island."

I closed my eyes and focused on the thread about my middle that pulled me northwest. The connection was strong. "It's that way. I can't feel precisely where it is, but well before the North Pole."

"All right then, we'll head that way. You can tell me when it's close? I don't want to run aground."

"Yes. It still feels miles off."

We stared silently out at the sea as the motor rumbled and waves slapped against the hull. Fog was starting to roll across the water, concealing the gray waves. The effect was eerie and added to the tension inside the pilothouse. I tried to keep from bouncing on my feet. No one needed to know how anxious I was. We could handle this. We'd survived a decade on the run. This was just one little hurdle. Get the scroll, destroy it. Risk averted.

But how could I destroy the scroll without Aidan realizing I'd done it on purpose? That would open me up to a lot of uncomfortable questions.

That was the one thing I hadn't figured out yet, and it scared the crap out of me.

"I'm going to head outside." I needed a minute to myself. "Can I just wave at you from the bow if I feel us getting closer?"

"Aye, that'll be fine," Captain Alden said. "Just be sure to stand at the very front where I can see you."

"All right." I hightailed it out of the pilothouse and down the stairs, taking them two at a time. I shook my arms, hoping to banish my nerves.

I crossed the rolling deck to the bow and found a spot beneath an overhang where I was pretty sure no one could see me. The captain was right above me. If I felt us nearing the island, I'd run a few feet to where he could see me and alert him. The biting wind cut through my jacket as I stared out at the water. The smell of the sea was strong, but not enough to block out Aidan's evergreen scent when he leaned against the wall next to me.

"Hey," he said.

"What's up?" I asked.

He handed me the paper package he'd been carrying earlier.

"What's this?"

"For you."

A gift? I tore open the paper and found a plain white box. When I opened it, two gleaming obsidian daggers rested inside.

My throat tightened. "What are these?"

"A replacement for your old pair. They're enchanted to return to you."

"How'd you get them? They're really rare."

"I'm also really wealthy."

"Yeah." I didn't know what else to say besides, "Thanks."

"I figured I owed you. You're helping me find the scroll. You shouldn't lose your favorite daggers as well."

"How'd you even find time?"

"I admit I didn't go out and get them myself. I—"

"Made a call."

"Yeah." He rubbed his hand over the back of his neck, almost as if he felt awkward. About his wealth?

"Have you always been like this? You know—private planes, people to do your bidding, that sort of thing?"

"No." He leaned against the wall next to me. "The Origin name may be famous, but that doesn't mean wealthy. I grew up poor. My dad died when I was young. He was the Origin before me. My mom raised me on her salary from two waitressing jobs. She did the best she could."

"Where is she now?"

"Died when I was eighteen. I was a mercenary for a few years. Then I got sick of having a boss. So I started Origin Enterprises."

"And what, just turned it into a multimillion-dollar organization?"

"It took a few years."

"Well, you clearly don't suck at it."

"You don't suck at what you do either." He shifted to stand in front of me. He blocked the wind as he loomed over me. Damn, he looked good. His voice was husky as he said, "We make a good team."

"Um...we're not a team." I didn't want to say it, but he was leaning down toward me and I panicked. His dark eyes devoured me, and his scent made my mouth water.

"We could be," he murmured.

My gaze was riveted to his lips. This was such a bad idea, but I wanted it. In a few hours, I'd walk away from him forever. What could one kiss hurt?

When he lowered his mouth to mine, I stood up on my toes and met him halfway. His lips were firm and warm. Heavenly. Kissing Aidan drowned out everything else. All I could smell and feel was him—his big arm wrapped around my waist, the heat and strength of his chest.

My head buzzed as his lips moved expertly on mine. I let him press me back against the wall and reached up to sink my free hand into his hair. It was so soft, a delicious contrast to his hard muscles. Desire heated my skin and coiled within me. I could let this go on forever.

He made a soft groan. The noise made me shiver, and I pressed closer to him, wanting to touch as much of him as I could.

My dragon sense tugged at me, stronger than ever. We were nearing the island. I didn't want to, but I pulled away from Aidan and slipped under his arm. My skin was still hot where he'd touched me and my lips tingled, but I tried to ignore it as I ran to the bow and waved my arms at the pilothouse.

Captain Alden caught sight of me immediately and nodded. The boat began to turn. I returned to Aidan.

"Time to go," I said.

"We'll finish this later." His dark gaze was determined, his jaw set.

There wouldn't be a later, but I couldn't say that. Instead, I hurried to the pilothouse.

"You still don't see anything?" I asked as I stepped in.

Everyone leaned towards the windows, peering out. I could feel Aidan close behind, but I tried to ignore what his nearness did to me.

"Nothing," Captain Alden said. "And it feels bloody strange here. Like we ought to turn around. You sure it's out there, lassie?"

"I know it is." The invisible string around my waist pulled hard. Unmistakable. But I was also getting that sense that we should turn around or divert our course. Anything to keep from going forward.

A spell, no doubt. Intended to hide the island from mariners by making them steer around. The fog made it feel like we were a ghost ship sailing through the mist.

"I'm not liking this one bit, lassie," Captain Alden said. Concern thickened his brogue. "We're going to have to turn the ship around."

The spell was getting stronger. My skin crawled with unease.

"It's a spell," I said. "Hiding the island."

"Even so, this fog is too thick to see land." Captain Alden waved his hand at the gray mist ahead of us. "We could run aground if we continue on."

Frustration welled in me.

"That's not an option," Aidan said. "We need to go forward."

"I can't risk the boat, lad."

"Can we have the rowboat?" I asked. "The one hanging off the back of the ship."

"And row alone into the mist?" Nix asked.

It didn't sound good when she put it like that. "We don't have a lot of choices."

She sighed. "No, we don't, do we?"

"Aye, you can have the rowboat," Captain Alden said. "We'll give you a radio in case you run into trouble. Though I can't guarantee we can get to you quickly. Not until this fog lifts."

"Del, do you think you'll be able to transport soon?" I asked. "And bring us along in case we get into trouble?"

"I should be. I feel almost at full power."

"That solves it, then," Captain Alden said. "O'Connel, get them set up with the rowboat. If you're not back in eight hours, I'll assume the lassie took you home. Good luck to you all."

I followed O'Connel, the deckhand, down the stairs. Aidan stayed behind, thanking the captain, and then joined us at the stern a minute later. The deckhand lowered the rowboat using pulleys as I removed Aidan's daggers from their box and slipped them into the sheaths at my thighs. They fit, though not perfectly. It'd have to do. I put my old ones into the box.

Once the rowboat was lowered to the water, I handed the box to the deckhand and asked, "Is there any chance you could ship this to Ancient Magic in Magic's Bend, Oregon? I'll pay you if you send your return address with it."

He nodded. "Not a problem." He took the box and nodded to the boat. "You can board. Good luck."

"Thanks." I climbed in after Nix and Del. The boat wobbled under my feet. It wasn't more than ten feet long—just a tiny thing meant for shore landings in shallow harbors.

Aidan climbed in last and took up the oars. Nix and Del sat in the back, leaning against each other. I huddled in the bow as the deckhand gave us a push that sent us drifting off into the mist.

CHAPTER THIRTEEN

Aidan's strokes cut powerfully through the water, the slap of the oars against the surface the only sounds.

"This is creepy," Nix muttered.

"Seconded," Del said.

Man, were they right. I could see nothing through the thick white fog, and the temperature felt like it was dropping. Not the natural kind of drop either—the kind that accompanied ghosts. But it was the sickening feeling in my stomach and the prickle that crawled across my skin that was the worst.

"Do you guys feel that?" I asked.

"The sense of extreme foreboding and that we should turn around immediately?" Aidan asked. "Yes."

"That's the one. But we're going the right way," I said, squinting into the fog. "I feel it."

I ignored the instincts that told me to turn around and stared into the mist. It was just magic. Aidan rowed as the rest of us huddled in the boat. My breathing cut through the silence.

"We're getting closer." I rubbed my arms, trying to keep the warmth in. "I can feel it."

"Sure can't see it, though," Nix said.

"We've got to be—"

The boat crashed into something, crunching against rock and spraying water into the air. I flew forward, but Aidan grabbed me before I went face-first into stone.

"We're taking on water!" Nix yelled.

Waves rocked the boat, heaving it against the rocks. Fog shrouded the boulders and stone ledges that rose up in front of us.

"This is it!" I called. "Get on land."

We scrambled out of the boat as it lurched against the rocks. Icy water splashed me and sharp stones dug into my hands as I scrambled onto solid ground. I turned to face the sea. Aidan and Nix stood next to me. Del leapt off the boat, which was going down fast.

"Not the easy beach landing I'd been hoping for," Aidan said.

"No." I watched the last of the boat sink under the waves and turned away from the misty sea. Jagged rocks rose up in front of me. "And this looks a hell of a lot like the creepy island in *King Kong.*"

"Seconded again," Del said.

"Let's make our way inland," Aidan said.

The rocks ahead tumbled over each other like giant stairs. I began to climb, using my hands to help me keep my footing. By the time we reached flat ground, much of the fog had dissipated. It still rolled over the ground like something out of a horror movie, but it stayed low enough that we could see ahead.

A brilliant orange sun hovered over the horizon, casting its glow on a village as it set. Brilliant. We'd be doing this in the dark soon.

"It still feels weird," I said, shivering against the sense of strange magic. It was old and dark and very unfamiliar. Possibly old enough to be unstable.

"Different," Aidan said. "Like there's dark magic here, but not like we have to turn around. It's not a diversion spell."

"I really hope that town isn't full of angry villagers," I muttered, gazing at the small settlement of old cottages that sat on the other side of the rolling field before us. It looked to be about a mile away. That was a long way to walk over ground that had no cover. If only Del didn't have to preserve her energy for emergencies, she could teleport us across. Looked like we were doing it the hard way.

"Seconded," Del said.

"We need to head to the village," I said.

We set off across the field. I felt like prey, as if being out in the open left me exposed and vulnerable. My senses twitched like mad, trying to pick out the scent and taste and feel of all the magic that surrounded me. There was so much of it that it was impossible to distinguish where or who it was coming from. So many scents hit my nose—most of them bad—and so many tastes enveloped my tongue that I almost gagged.

I drew my knives and said, "This place is wild. Can you feel the magic?"

"Yeah," Aidan said. "But I can't sense who it's coming from."

"Me neither," Del said.

"If it's the thief's protective magic, he's going a good job," Nix added.

For real. If my life hadn't been on the line with the information that scroll contained, I'd have hightailed it out of here. When I sensed magic, it usually came from another person. But I saw no one.

We were about halfway across the scrubby field when the ground began to tremble. I stumbled. The scent of dark magic grew—like rotting earth. The ground shook harder.

"Hurry," I said as I picked up the pace. We needed to get away from here. The magic was strengthening. I could feel it seething and roiling beneath our feet.

"Run," Aidan said.

We picked up the pace, sprinting across the vibrating dirt. My lungs burned as I raced away from whatever threatened us. The earth groaned loudly, an unholy noise that broke the silence.

An enormous crack opened in front of me, a fissure reaching into the dark earth. Aidan grabbed my arm as I stopped abruptly at the edge, teetering over the abyss.

He yanked me back onto solid ground, but the sound of the earth breaking echoed around us. Cracks streaked across the soil. Dark magic wafted up from them, smelling strongly of the rotting earth I'd noticed before.

We were surrounded on all sides by deep fissures that looked like they led to hell. Fear chilled my skin. Would we make it only this far?

Aidan threw out his hands and the scent of his evergreen magic washed over me. Magic burst from his palms, a shimmer of light directed at the field ahead. The earth trembled and groaned as it pushed itself together, building a safe path for us.

"This way!" Aidan yelled over the sound of breaking earth. He sprinted along the path he'd created. We followed, racing in a line along the narrow bridge of land. Crevices continued to open on all sides of us as we ran.

My lungs burned as I sucked in air tainted with rancid magic. I glanced behind to see our path cracking open once more.

No going back.

Ahead of us, Aidan continued to build a path with his magic. We neared the village. When we stumbled onto a street that dead-ended at the field, silence fell abruptly. The sound of groaning earth ceased.

I spun to face the field.

It looked normal.

"What the hell?" I wheezed, bracing myself on my knees as I caught my breath. Nix did the same, though Del looked fine. She'd always been the most athletic.

Aidan looked completely unfazed by the sprint as he said, "Our magic ignited the field. Whatever dark magic enchants it came to life."

And now it was dormant again. Though I could still smell the rotting earth, another scent hit me as I turned to face the village street. It was fresh and so icy it chilled my nose.

"Weird magic here, too," I said.

We stood on a short, dirt street. Only two small cottages on either side. With their decaying thatch roofs, thick stone walls, and tiny windows, they looked to be at least a few hundred years old. The orange flame of the setting sun glinted off the thick glass in the windows.

Nix peered into one, then jerked back. "It looks like people are home. There's food on the table."

A chill crawled over my skin as I approached the window. This was so horror movie it wasn't even funny. Aidan was peering in, so I nudged him aside and peeked for myself.

Nix was right. The small cottage had a rough, wooden table set for three. The old wooden bowls were full of some sort of stew and a great pot hung over the hearth. The flame was dead though.

"No one's in there," Aidan said.

"I don't think they have been for a long time," I said. "This place feels abandoned. But it smells like magic."

When a ghostly form floated out of the wall, the familiar misery hit me. It poked at my mind with sharp claws, searching for my worst memories. The ghostly figure was a woman wearing a regal gown, her hair done up elaborately and styled with jewels. She shimmered a transparent silvery blue, the shadows under her eyes standing out starkly. When her lips parted, I saw fangs.

"FireSoul," she hissed.

I shuddered. Another drifted out of the wall beside her.

"Phantoms," I breathed as I backed away from the window. That was the icy smell. Thank fate that Aidan couldn't hear what they said about me.

"They aren't normal Phantoms," Aidan said as he backed away. "That one was vampire."

Extra creepy. I'd never heard of a vampire Phantom.

"Do you think they evicted the residents of the island?" Nix asked.

"Probably," Aidan said. "There's all kinds of wild magic here. Something strange happened to this place."

"Something evil," I said. I could feel it.

"Let's get a move on," Del said.

I tried to ignore the cold and the piercing pain in my head as we set off down the short street. It spilled onto a larger one that had houses on each side. The town's main road, presumably. Though it was a bit generous to call it a town. The street stretched several hundred yards in both directions, and every building was as small and shabby as the one we'd peered into. It was more of a village than a town, presided over by the large manor house at the end of the road. The huge building called to my dragon sense.

"Toward the manor house," I said.

Mist crept along the ground as we turned right. I clutched my knives, ready for whatever came at us. My head still ached from the Phantom, and I was afraid they weren't done with us yet. Del's sword hung loosely at her side, as did Nix's. As usual, Aidan didn't carry a weapon.

When the ghostly forms drifted through the walls of the houses and out onto the street, I tensed, bracing myself for more pain as they reached inside my mind.

They were dressed in all manner of historic outfits—from the gowns of regal ladies to armor of knights and the motley of jesters. All glowed with icy blue light.

How long had they been here? How hungry were they to feed on another's misery?

"Hurry!" I broke into a run.

The sun was nearly set, the street now lit by the Phantoms' eerie glow. It cast a blue light on everything around us.

The ghostly figures drifted away from the walls of the houses, reaching for us. I winced as I felt their dark, icy magic reach inside my mind, searching out my worst memories. Pain seared as my brain rejected them. Even the Phantoms couldn't get at my memories.

"FireSoul," they hissed.

When one dressed like a queen grabbed my arm, I shrieked in surprise. It felt like an icy blade sliced me.

She wasn't supposed to be able to touch! Phantoms worked only with memories and fear.

I swiped at the hand with my dagger, but it only passed through. The feel of my knuckles grazing its cloak burned like acid poured on an open wound.

Nix shrieked in pain as one grabbed her arm. She lashed out with her blade, but it too passed right through the Phantom.

Ten feet ahead, more silvery bodies formed a barricade at the end of the street, blocking the manor. On either side of us, Phantoms closed in, reaching out with silvery claws.

"We'll have to run through them!" I said.

"We can't," Aidan said. His face was twisted with pain. "It'll tear us apart."

From the searing pain that hit me wherever they touched, I believed him.

"Turn into a griffon!" I shouted.

"Can't." His voice was tight with pain. "The Phantoms stop me."

"My blades don't work!" I shrunk back as they closed in. They surrounded us like a pack of snarling wolves, their faces ravenous for misery and their claws outstretched. My head hurt so badly that I could barely see straight. We had only seconds before they converged upon us with their blade-like touch.

One grabbed Del and pulled her into the crowd. It wrapped its arms fully around her body, enveloping her fully. Her eyes widened, but she didn't scream in pain. But being touched by so many should be excruciating.

Del began to fade, turning a slivery blue.

"No!" I screamed, lunging toward her.

They couldn't turn Del into one of them. Not my *deirfiúr*. That shouldn't even be possible. But she had turned silvery blue, and her blade glowed like cobalt flame.

The three of us attacked the Phantoms that surrounded Del. I plunged my blades into the first one I came to, trying to beat my way to her. They flew straight through, and I had to pull back before I stabbed myself in the thighs. The feeling of my arms plunging through the transparent body was like being sliced by a thousand icy knives.

The Phantom grabbed me, wrapping its arms around my waist as the other had done with Del. The feel of thousands of knives slicing my skin was excruciating. I shrieked.

No! I didn't want to be a Phantom, cursed to haunt this island for eternity.

Through blurry vision and searing pain, I realized that my skin wasn't turning transparent silvery blue as Del's had done. Near me, Nix and Aidan were struggling in the arms of other Phantoms. Tears poured down Nix's face, but she still looked human. Aidan as well.

Only Del was blue.

Del swiped out with her sword, severing the arm of a Phantom. It screamed and collapsed.

Holy magic, Del was part Phantom. Del's sword moved like lightning as she cut down the Phantoms nearest her. From behind, she beheaded the one that clutched Nix and jabbed her blade into the shoulder of the Phantom who held Aidan. They released their prey. Del lunged at me, plunging her blade into the side of my Phantom.

"Run!" she screamed.

"Not without you!"

"I'm coming." She beheaded another Phantom with a swipe of her sword. "Go!"

More Phantoms converged on us, reaching out with clawed hands. Del could fight better without us in the way. I ran.

I hated to leave her, but knew I had to. We all had specific battle skills—apparently, this was one of Del's.

The three of us sprinted down the street toward the great garden that stretched out in front of the manor house on the hill. A tall stone wall and a wrought iron gate marked the end of the street and the beginning of the palatial property. My lungs burned as we raced for it.

Aidan reached the gate first, Nix just behind him. He stopped and turned, kneeling on the ground and cupping his hands in front of him to provide a step for her.

Without stopping, Nix stepped onto his hands and he vaulted her up. She grabbed the top of the tall gate and scrambled over, dropping onto the other side.

Just as I reached him, Aidan knelt and did the same for me. With a long stride, I planted my left foot in his hands and he heaved me upward. I seized the gate and pulled myself over. Aidan leapt over a second later.

I collapsed on the ground, aching and panting. I gripped the gate bars, watching Del fight with my heart lodged in my throat. She fought like a woman possessed, all those years as a demon hunter paying off. Her silvery blue hair whipped as she spun around and cut straight through the waist of a Phantom who reached for her. Her eyes glowed bright with rage and she turned on another, her blade flashing like blue flame.

"I can change now that I'm away from them," Aidan said. "I'll go get her as a griffon."

I shook my head. "It looks like she's got this in the bag."

Del had always been a good fighter—stronger and faster than most Magica—but her Phantom speed was insane.

And she looked pissed as she swung her blade.

"No, I'm getting her," Aidan said. His magic swelled around him, evergreen and chocolate flooding my senses.

I reached out a hand and grabbed his arm, never taking my eyes off Del. "Seriously, she wouldn't want you to."

I hoped she wasn't stuck as a Phantom forever. But if she was, she'd want to be the one to kill every last one that had turned her. Being *rescued* by Aidan halfway through having her vengeance would just piss her the hell off.

"Fine." Aidan's voice was clipped, but I didn't give a crap if he was displeased. I was too busy being worried about and impressed by Del.

She slaughtered the last Phantom and stood, her sword hanging at her side. She glowed a pale silvery blue as she surveyed the carnage. Then she turned and walked toward us, her steps deliberate and her face set.

I glanced at Nix. "She looks like a freaking badass."

"Seriously," Nix breathed. "She needs a superhero name."

Del neared the gate and we stood. Instead of climbing over, she walked straight through the bars.

If I hadn't been so scared the change was permanent, I'd have complimented her on her awesome new gifts. Instead, I said, "What the hell happened?"

"No idea," Del said. Slowly, she was turning corporeal again. The blue tint to her skin faded, replaced by her normal skin tone. She looked down at her hand. A relieved sigh heaved out of her. "Oh, thank fate."

I reached out and touched her hand. She felt normal.

"So, no one here knows why Del just turned into a Phantom?" Aidan asked.

We shook our heads.

"No idea," I said as I turned and got my first good look at the garden. "But we'll have to figure it out later, because I think this garden is gonna be a problem."

The moon and stars were bright, shining down on the garden that stretched out on either side of the narrow road that led up the long sloping hill. At the top of the hill sat the elaborate manor house. In moonlight, it looked like a crouching dragon. Statues of mythical beasts lined the drive. Behind them, wild topiaries of animals snarled.

"Who the heck maintains this place?" Nix asked.

"No one," I said as the garden's magic washed over me. There were dozens of scents and tastes—so much magic running amok, some of it decaying from age. As if it weren't controlled by a Magica, but by itself. "The magic feels old and strange. It's decayed and some has gone wild."

"Our thief lives here?" Del asked. "Verrry depressing."

"It's great from a security perspective," Aidan said. "If you're a wanted criminal, this island does a damn good job of keeping you hidden and deterring those who're after you. All the thief has to do is transport straight into the house."

Good point. If this thief had been filling his house up with treasure for years, it had to be awesome. I itched to explore.

"Follow the yellow brick road?" I asked.

"Only if I get to be Dorothy," Aidan said.

I glanced at him. He loomed beside me, his shoulders broad and his face intensely masculine. "You would never pass for a Dorothy."

"Fair enough," he said.

I drew my blades, and we set off up the road. The air tingled with magic, prickling against my skin. Actually, it felt like a lot of things—bugs crawling, blowing sand, slimy cold. All of them bad.

We'd only made it past the first pair of stone statues when the magic changed. It surged to life, vibrating on the air.

"We triggered the magic," I said. Just like in one of my tombs.

Stone creaked and groaned on either side of us. Two great, horned beasts with bulging stone muscles jumped down from their pedestals. The ground vibrated beneath their hooves.

Stone minotaurs. They each raised an enormous clawed hand to obliterate us.

CHAPTER FOURTEEN

Del swiped out with her sword, aiming for the arm of the one closest to her. Metal bounced off stone.

"Shit!" She jumped back.

Well, my daggers wouldn't stand a chance.

Aidan threw out his hand and blasted magic at the minotaur on his side of the road. It ricocheted off. "Damn it. Their stone is enchanted against my control."

Damn. If the Elemental Mage couldn't control these lumps of rock, we were screwed.

Nix held out her hand. Light glowed and the flowery scent of her magic washed over me. A huge mallet appeared. She gripped it with both hands and swung it at the minotaur who was closing in on her.

He shattered beneath the blow.

"Nice," I said.

She tossed me the enormous mallet. I caught it. "Oof."

Weighed a ton. I swung it at the other minotaur as she conjured three more and handed them off. We set off down the road, swinging our mallets at the stone beasts that came to life. Monsters of all shapes and sizes shattered at our feet.

"This is pretty fun!" I said as I swung at a two-headed snake that rose high above me. My arms shook when the mallet collided with stone, but the monster shattered into a hundred pieces.

Got him!

An enraged roar vibrated my eardrums. Hot breath blew from behind, wafting my hair in front of my face.

Oh, holy magic, I'd spoken too soon.

Dread soured my gut as I turned and stared into the green eyes of an enormous three headed dog. Like Cerberus.

He looked like the topiary I'd just seen.

Come to life?

His breath reeked of rotten meat and his fangs dripped yellow slime. I stumbled back and raised my mallet, but it was laughably small compared to the monstrous dog.

Behind him, other topiary beasts shook themselves and shed their leaves to become monstrous animals. Winged serpents, giant alligators, and raging hippos burst to life, their growls rumbling through the night.

"Oh, holy magic, we're screwed," I breathed.

Gold flashed at the corner of my eye, then a horrifying roar broke through the beasts' growls. I whirled to face it.

Aidan was a griffon.

He was the one who had roared.

Damn, he was scary.

Aidan crouched low, then launched himself into the air. He roared at Cerberus again. Cerberus bowed his head low. It looked a hell of a lot like a gesture of respect. Cerberus then turned and ran, his giant strides eating up the ground. With a giant leap, he cleared the stone fence and disappeared into the night.

Something hard crashed into my shoulder and knocked me to the ground. Pain shot through my shoulder. An enormous stone werewolf loomed over me, his hunched back and giant wolfish head unmistakable. He wasn't the real sort of werewolf shifter, but rather the fantasy kind. The extra-scary, monster kind.

He swiped out with his huge stone claws, and I rolled to escape, then scrambled to my feet. I grabbed my mallet and swung, hitting him in the shoulder.

Aidan's roar rent the night again as half of the werewolf exploded. I swung again, aiming for the other side. My shoulder screamed in pain as my mallet crashed against stone, but the werewolf finally burst into a pile of rubble.

I glanced skyward. Aidan swept through the night, roaring at the topiaries as they shook themselves to life. They bowed immediately, then took off.

On either side of me, Nix and Del fought stone monsters that animated as soon as we crossed their pedestals. At least they all didn't come to life at once.

As soon as the thought crossed my mind, the magic in the air swelled. It battered my senses, a hundred awful scents and tastes at once. Ahead of me, the remaining statues burst to life even though we weren't anywhere near them.

"The magic is mutating!" I shouted. It was responding to our threat and changing to meet it.

"I hate smart magic," Del grunted as she slammed her mallet into the side of a two-headed goat monster.

Maybe the thief hadn't enchanted this island to remain hidden from mariners. Maybe the island had enchanted itself as the magic had aged.

Great.

The stone monsters charged us. I glanced skyward again. Aidan was still subduing the giant topiary beasts. If he stopped to help us, those monsters would come from behind and devour us.

It was up to the three of us to beat our way to the house. Nix and Del charged the stone monsters, swinging their mallets with precision. I joined them, trying to ignore the pain in my shoulder. Rocks exploded into the air as our blows landed.

By the time we'd destroyed the last stone monster, Del and Nix were both limping and my arm hung uselessly at my side.

"Oh, my ribs," Del moaned. "Definitely cracked a few."

She leaned against me as we waited for Aidan to finish demanding obedience from the giant beasts. Nix thumped to the ground and rubbed her calf.

"Those stone bastards packed a hell of a punch," she muttered.

"Good thinking with the mallets," I said. "They were special, right?"

She nodded. "A modification of Thor's hammer."

I looked down at my mallet—excuse me, hammer—with more respect. Nix couldn't create conjurations that had magic, but if there was magic around her, she could put it into her conjuration—like she'd done with the chalice that we now hunted. She must have taken some of the crazy magic in this place and created a version of Thor's hammer.

"Badass," I said.

"Thanks." She climbed to her feet as Aidan landed in front of us.

In a swirl of golden light, he turned back into a man.

"Damn," Del said. "I'd kinda hoped you'd end up naked."

He grinned. "Not since I was a pup."

"Ah well." She shrugged.

I tried not to think of him naked. What was wrong with me? Even in the middle of this situation, I couldn't help myself.

I turned to face the manor house. It loomed over us, creepier up close than it had been from far away. It had dozens of mullioned windows, ornate cornices, and stonework arches. The sort just perfect for mean little pixies to hide within. Expansive stone steps led up to a pair of enormous black doors. Even the stone appeared black in the moonlight, and the windows were dark.

"Think our guy is inside?" Aidan asked.

"I feel him coming from that direction, so probably." I started up the stairs.

"Excellent," he said. "When we come upon him, let's attack from different directions. Cass and I, Del and Nix."

"Okay," I said.

"Those mallets should take care of the doors, then," he said.

"Not a chance," Nix said. "No point in using a hammer when we can use a key."

We reached the landing, and Nix leaned her mallet against the wall. I held on to mine because I liked it. It wouldn't do for my normal work—I didn't want to be smashing my way through temples and tombs—but it was fun for now.

Nix held her palm out facing upward and touched the lock with her other hand. A blue glow enveloped both her hands. A moment later, it faded, leaving behind a golden key in her upturned palm.

"This should do it." She slipped it into the lock and turned. *Snick.*

She pushed it open. The door creaked as it swung, like we were entering a haunted house.

Of course.

The dry air that rolled out smelled like neglect and abandonment. As we stepped into the large foyer, the feeling only intensified. I pulled my lightstone from my jacket and shoved it onto my finger. Del did the same with hers. Nix didn't carry one, but it was more than enough light to illuminate the foyer.

It was an elegant space, with marble floors and a soaring ceiling. An enormous chandelier hung overhead, and a sweeping staircase ascended to the second floor. Enormous paintings hung on the wall, and marble statues dotted alcoves.

Fortunately, they didn't come to life. But the stain of old dark magic dripped down the walls.

"Fancy," Del muttered.

"Very," I said. "But I don't think he lives here. There's almost no magic. Just the shadow of it." I pointed toward the ceiling where the shadow of magic dripped like tar down the walls.

I'd expected more wild magic within the house. Instead, it felt almost peaceful. I shivered as an awful feeling rolled over me. It was peaceful, but not in a nice way.

"Feels like death," Aidan said.

I couldn't agree more. There was something dark here. Far darker than the magic that had enchanted the garden or allowed the foreign Phantoms to set up shop in the village. Not just magic that had died, but something worse.

"We shouldn't stay here long," Aidan said. "Which way, Cass?"

"Ahead. Toward the back of the house."

We crossed the marble foyer, keeping our footsteps silent. We hesitated at the double doors. I propped my mallet against the wall and drew my knives. As much as I loved the mallet, my knives were better against the thief. If he was on the other side of this door, I wanted to be ready.

We nodded at each other, then slipped through the doors. The room on the other side was empty. An enormous dining room stretched out before us. My light glinted off the suits of armor lining the long room. Normally, I'd expect them to come to life.

Here, I wasn't worried. Animated armor was almost sweet compared to the feeling that pervaded this house. If despair had a smell or a taste, it would be what I was currently sensing.

I jerked my head toward the door on the other side of the room, and my comrades nodded. We skirted around the long table, which was still set with an elaborate meal. Though it looked fresh, I'd guess it'd been there for centuries.

We hesitated at this door as well. At Aidan's signal, we pushed it open and went through.

Nothing.

Just an empty sunroom dotted with chaise lounges and settees. The large glass windows looked out on a partially destroyed cathedral. My dragon sense tugged hard.

"In there." I pointed at the cathedral.

"Why the hell is he in there? That's almost spookier than this house," Nix whispered.

She was right. The cathedral was built entirely of stone. It was far too big for an island this size. The walls soared high, crumbling here and there. The roof was long gone and so was the glass, leaving empty spaces in the ornate stone walls.

"He's definitely in there," I said. My dragon sense was pulling harder than ever, which often happened when I neared my prey.

"This place is freaking weird, and this thief is freaking weird," Del said.

"We'll split up," Aidan said. "Enter from different sides."

"Good idea," I said.

He looked at me. "You and I will go from the left, Del and Nix from the right. The way those walls are crumbling, it won't be hard to find an entrance. We'll go quickly across the grass and enter the cathedral sixty seconds from when we leave this room."

I nodded. My *deirfiúr* both said, "Agreed."

Del and I both looked at our watches, then nodded at our partners. We all slipped out the door and raced across the grass, veering off to head for our assigned sides of the cathedral. Aidan loped ahead of me, his long legs carrying him farther faster.

The moon shined brightly, illuminating our path. I prayed to magic that the thief wasn't looking out a window. And that he didn't have guards on the lookout.

Aidan and I leapt over a fallen column and sidled up to the cathedral wall. We edged over to a gap in the stone. I glanced at my watch, then up at Aidan and mouthed, "Five seconds."

I peeked around the edge of the wall and into the space. The cathedral was empty, the floor grown over with grass. Movement caught my eye from the front. A dark-haired man stalked back and forth, a black bag at his feet. The thief. He looked like he was waiting for something.

He whirled toward us, as if he sensed something. Our sixty seconds were up and I had a clear line of sight, so I flung a dagger at him.

Quick as a flash, he threw up his hand, and a bolt of lightning knocked the dagger away. Thunder boomed, vibrating my chest, and the scent of ozone rent the air.

I lunged backward. Holy magic, I'd never seen anyone throw lightning before.

Aidan surged into the room. He used his magic to lift a fallen column off the ground. It hurtled through the air at the thief. Again, the Lightning Mage threw a sparking white bolt. Aidan lunged behind the wall.

The column exploded, the sound vibrating my eardrums. The smell of singed stone burned my nostrils.

How the hell were we supposed to fight this guy? He had lightning.

"Use your powers," Aidan demanded. "You're a damned Mirror Mage. Blast him back."

"I could kill us all!" I looked back into the room in time to see Del and Nix enter from behind the thief.

Nix had conjured lightning rods and placed them a dozen feet in front of them, like a shield. As they advanced, she conjured more lightning rods, an ever-extending field of protection.

Until the Lightning Mage whirled around and saw what faced him. He laughed, a dark sound, then flicked his hand. Another fallen column rose into the air and battered down the lightning rods. The thief threw an enormous bolt of lightning at them that cracked through the air.

It parted and arced up, forming a domed cage of lightning over my *deirfiúr*. Trapped.

"No!" Enraged and terrified, I raced into the cathedral. I had to stop him before he killed them. I raised my knife to hurl it as the thief spun around. He raised a hand and launched an enormous bolt of lightning at me.

One crystal thought flashed in my mind. *I'm dead because I didn't use my magic.*

Something enormous crashed into my back, throwing me to the ground behind a column, blocking me from the lightning. Pain blossomed in my injured shoulder as I rolled to see the lightning strike Aidan, who'd become a griffon. He lit up like a lightbulb, shaking, then collapsed, his huge form limp.

I gasped and reached for him.

Oh, fates, not Aidan. He'd thrown himself in front of lightning for me. He couldn't be dead.

But he looked it.

More than anything, I wanted to go to him. But if I did, we were all dead.

They relied on me.

And the only chance I had was to use my magic. I couldn't beat this guy with knives or quickness. Oh, fates, I didn't want to blow us all up. If I tried to use lightning, that wasn't outside the realm of possibilities.

But my *deirfiúr* were in that cage and Aidan lay dead or dying.

I blew out a shaky breath, then opened myself up to the thief's magic. It sparked and crackled as it washed over me, lighting me up in a way that made me feel entirely alive. I absorbed it, picturing myself as a lightning rod.

When I felt full to bursting with electricity, I tried to gather it up, to harness it. The scent of ozone filled my nose. I envisioned myself throwing a bolt of lightning right at him, then popped up from behind the column.

He was striding toward me. I threw out my hands and released the lightning.

It went awry, an enormous bolt hitting one wall. The stone exploded and crumbled, throwing dust into the air.

Damn! I dived behind the column again. Fortunately, the rocks had missed my *deirfiúr* and Aidan. But they'd also missed the thief, who'd been thrown to the side. I seriously doubted he was dead.

My entire body shook as I tried to harness the lightning again. I envisioned less of it. It'd be easier to control, and maybe I'd keep him alive long enough to ask some questions. How had he found me? Why did he want me?

Once I had a grasp on the lightning, I peered up over the column. He was climbing to his feet from where he'd been thrown. I stood, but before I could throw the lightning, he caught sight of me. His dark eyes blazed as he threw a bolt.

I dived to the side, barely missing being struck by it. I lunged up and threw my bolt at him, praying.

It hit him square in the chest. He shook and fell, his body alight.

I sprinted to him. It'd been a small bolt. Was he dead?

I skidded to a stop near him and straddled him, my hands around his throat. They hit a thick metal collar, but it didn't strike me as odd when I felt his magic. He was alive. Which I could have guessed since his electric cage still buzzed over my *deirfiúr*. It should fade when he died.

He looked young—not more than twenty. He had black eyes and would have been handsome if his magic didn't feel so awful—dark and polluted. It washed over me. It felt like drowning in tar made up of people's evilest impulses. Though strangely, it didn't feel connected to him. Like it was separate. It made no sense.

I shook him. "What do you know about me?"

His eyes fluttered open, then widened.

"FireSoul," he hissed.

"How do you know?"

He just laughed. His dark magic pulsed, making me want to retch. It felt like it reached inside of me and twined about my insides, squeezing.

"Tell me or I'll kill you," I demanded.

"You kill me, he kills me. What's the difference? It would be a blessing."

"Who is *he*? Do you work for someone?"

His black eyes rolled in his head. "He hunts you. You are the hunted now, Huntress."

"How do you know that name?" Only my *deirfiúr* knew that name. I shook him hard and he coughed.

"The scroll," he wheezed. "I read it. Master will be pleased to know where you are."

"Master? Who the hell is that? Why does he want to know where I am?" Fear chilled my skin.

"Master hunts us all." He stared up at me with blank eyes.

"All?"

"All of us. FireSouls."

Us? It hit me then, with sickening clarity. The collar. His immense power. He was an enslaved FireSoul.

Possibly enslaved by the man from my nightmare—the one who'd kept me in that dark stone room.

It was monstrous.

My gaze caught on his collar. There was a large latch on the front. It enraged me.

I pushed on the latch. The collar popped off.

He sucked in a harsh breath. The dark magic that had pulsed from him surged from the collar, washing over his body. Suddenly, his own magic felt purer, cleaner. It smelled like the desert and tasted like oranges. But the tar of the dark magic still covered it, sick and evil. His skin darkened, turning gray, as if the evil magic within him were rising to the surface.

"Does he know where I am?" I asked.

His gaze met mine. His eyes had changed from black to blue. And they were clearer. As if his mind were no longer fogged by the collar.

"No," he whispered. "Why he…needs the scroll. To find more of us."

"But you were in my shop."

"Not for you. For the chalice. He wants it. Shadow demon failed… He sent me to track it. I did not know what you were…until I read the scroll." He was gasping between words now.

"You haven't told him about me, then?" My heart beat so hard it tried to break my ribs.

"Was going to tonight…when he meets me."

"He meets you here?"

He jerked his head in assent. "Not allowed at his compound. FireSouls find the treasure, bring it here. He meets us. He doesn't…want us knowing where he is. But now, never have to see him again. Thank you."

"For what?"

"Death. Removing the collar."

"That killed you?" Horror welled in my chest. I'd killed him by removing it?

"No. It's…good. I was dead as soon as he put it on me. He can find me anywhere with it, but removing it releases the dark magic. Poisons me…" A hacking cough wracked him. He sucked in a ragged breath. "But you freed me. I wanted to take it off, but I couldn't. Forbidden…impossible for me to remove myself. But you've given me a gift."

His life had been so terrible that he believed this was a gift? "I'm so sorry."

"Don't be. I'll be free. There is no other way to be free once you wear the collar."

My mind spun with the horror of what he was saying.

"I can help you. Get you a healer," I said. "My friend heals."

"There is no healing this."

He was right. The gray was rising closer to the surface of his skin now. I could still feel his magic—bright and pure—but it was failing to keep the darkness from taking him.

"Take my magic," he said. "Use it to save yourself."

Tears burned my eyes. "What?"

"You've killed me, FireSoul. Now take my magic. My gift…to you."

A lump rose in my throat. I didn't want to. It felt dirty—not his magic, but the act of stealing from him as he died. I didn't want to take someone else's magic, much less that of a boy whom I'd killed.

"He comes for you," he wheezed. "You need strength. You must fight. Take it."

I sobbed, tears blurring my vision. "But I killed you."

"You have to. Make my death mean something. Use my power to defeat him. He comes for you... Even without the scroll, he will find you."

I sucked in a shuddering breath. He was right. I didn't want to take his power. I didn't want to become a true FireSoul. But this boy wasn't bad. He wasn't evil. What had enslaved him was evil. What hunted me was evil.

And he was dying. So I'd make his death count. I'd use his power to save myself and my *deirfiúr*. To defeat what came for us.

"What's your name?" I asked.

"Aaron."

"Thank you, Aaron."

He nodded.

"How do I do it?" I asked.

"You've already killed me. Now you must be the flame. Make a channel for the power to pass. Light us up."

"I'm not an Elemental Mage. I have no fire."

"Yes, FireSoul, you do. It is within you. It is you."

It is me? I closed my eyes and tried to clear my mind, to seek out and feel the power that was within me. I'd repressed it so long that at first it felt wrong. Dangerous. My heartbeat pounded in my ears, competing with the sound of Aaron's ragged breaths. Tears rolled down my cheeks at the knowledge of what I was doing.

"Try harder," Aaron croaked. "Use your fire."

I didn't know what that meant. I pictured fire, imagined its heat and flicker. The flame I saw in my mind's eye was a shimmering white. It was my flame. It was *me*.

Slowly, I felt it build. The flickering white flame filled my body, warm and growing hotter. It filled my chest and then my limbs, until finally it escaped and crawled across my skin.

"It's hot," I breathed. It was starting to hurt.

"Nothing is without price," Aaron said.

I opened my eyes. Aaron's face was peaceful. White flame flowed from me, extending out to him. It enveloped him, making him transparent enough to see through.

"Now take," Aaron said. "Lightning is my root power. That will become yours."

The flame was starting to really burn. I had to hurry. My power reached out for his, searching for the signature of lightning. I felt the dark magic poisoning him and tried not to gag. My magic skirted around it, reaching into his soul. It was pure and bright there, entirely separate from the dark magic I'd initially felt from him.

When I felt his sense of peace—the relief he felt at this moment of death—tears of gratitude rolled down my cheeks. I hated that his life had brought him to this, but I was so grateful he was content now. I could never steal the gifts of an unwilling supernatural. It would destroy me.

Finally, the feel of his lightning butted up against my magic. I'd found it, deep in his soul.

It crackled and burned, electric in its intensity. My magic twined with it as my flame grew higher around us. The pain of the fire turned to the spark of magic. Aaron's lightning traveled across the fire—a conduit, I realized—and found its way into my soul.

Inside my chest, the lightning jumped and crackled. The burning pain of the flame had faded, and I felt electric.

"Thank you," Aaron breathed.

I opened my eyes. He was gone. Stone still and lifeless, I could no longer feel even the dark magic that had polluted his body.

"I'm sorry, Aaron." I collapsed next to him and lay by his side. Though my chest felt full of electric magic, my muscles felt like jello. Too much magic in too short a time.

But I couldn't stay like this. Aaron's master was coming here to meet him. There was no way I could defeat him like this. We had to get out of here or my *deirfiúr* and I would end up like Aaron.

I pushed myself up. The lightning cage that had trapped Del and Nix had disappeared. They lay on their backs. Aidan was still on the ground as well.

Fear pushed the feel of the lightning out of my chest. I crawled over to Nix and Del. They were so pale, their dark hair spread out around their heads and their weapons lying useless at their sides. Their clothes were singed.

"Nix! Del!" I shook Del's shoulder.

She moaned and opened her eyes. "I feel like crap," she croaked.

"We're going to feel worse if we don't get out of here. Can you transport us?"

Weakly, she raised herself into a sitting position. "I think so. Just give me a second."

"Okay." I took one look at Nix to make sure she was only passed out—which she was, thank fates—and then crawled over to Aidan.

Sometime while I'd been with Aaron, Aidan had transformed back into a man. My hand trembled as I pressed my fingers to the pulse at his throat. Steady, but faint. I nearly collapsed in relief. He would live.

He was sprawled across the stone floor, easily two hundred pounds. We weren't going to be able to carry him. I'd deal with that in a minute, though. I had only a bit of strength left—enough to destroy the scroll or to borrow Aidan's gift and heal my friends. They could be healed after Del transported us home, but the scroll needed to be destroyed now, before Aidan woke. It was ruthless, but it had to be done.

I pushed myself up and staggered over to the black bag that lay near Aaron. It was a crumpled black gym bag—not nearly impressive enough to contain what it did. That little bit of humanity made a lump rise in my throat.

I picked it up and undid the zipper. An unimpressive scroll of vellum and the two chalices were inside. I wanted to open the scroll and see exactly what it said about me, but we had no time. Aaron's master could arrive any minute. We should take the scroll back and destroy it at Ancient Magic, but I wanted to be able to tell Aidan that it had been destroyed in the lightning battle and hadn't made it back with us. Besides, this was the perfect place for my brand of destructive magic. I couldn't burn all this stone.

Del appeared beside me. She leaned heavily on my shoulder. "Is it in there?"

"Yes. I'm going to try to destroy it." I withdrew the scroll and threw it on the ground about ten feet in front of me, then glanced at her. "You might want to back up."

She stepped back.

For the second time today, I tried to access my magic. It felt a bit more natural this time, but still foreign. Even trying to use it made my heart pound. I'd trained myself to repress it for so long that this felt entirely wrong.

I closed my eyes and focused on the magic within myself, letting it unfurl in my chest. It woke with a bang, rolling over me, as if it had been waiting years to be willingly released. I suppose it had been. I'd used it before—but only in unconscious moments of panic. Though I was freaked out right now, I was still consciously accessing my magic.

It felt strange and natural at the same time. But above all, necessary.

Flame would be needed to destroy the scroll. I reached for the flame that Aaron had taught me how to use. I felt the snap and crackle, smelled the scent of burning wood. I gathered it up and molded it, then released it in a great jet of fire that enveloped the scroll.

The fire roared, casting a glow on the cathedral walls. When it faded, I had to squint through the dark.

The scroll remained, lying untouched on the singed grass.

"Oh, shit," Del said. "It's protected."

Damn it. "I'll try one more thing, then we've got to get out of here."

I reached for the spark of lightning inside me. As I had before, I envisioned myself as a lightning rod. When I had collected enough, I released a bolt at the scroll.

Thunder boomed and the lightning lit up the night with a harsh white light. Instead of one direct bolt aimed at the scroll, two burst from my hands. One struck the corner of the cathedral, crumbling it, and the other bounced off the scroll.

Double damn. I might have finally accepted being a FireSoul and taken someone's powers, but I was still crap with my magic.

"It's not going to work," I told her. "We'll figure it out at home. We've gotta get out of here."

I grabbed the gym bag off the ground and raced to the scroll. It was cool to the touch when I picked it up—damned thing—and tossed it into the gym bag.

"Help me carry Nix," Del said. "She's easier than Aidan."

I slung the bag over my shoulder and ran to where she stood by Nix. I took Nix's feet while Del took her shoulders, and we carried our limp *deirfiúr's* body over to Aidan.

"Like old times," I muttered to Del.

She gave a wry laugh. "I was glad those time were over."

We'd gotten in a lot of scraps as girls on the run. Thieving meant sometimes running into supernaturals more powerful than ourselves. Until we'd learned to fight well, two of us often were left to carry the third to safety.

Gently, we placed Nix on the ground next to Aidan. I stood, then caught sight of Aaron's body.

"I can't just leave him here," I said.

"Uh, isn't he the bad guy?" Del asked.

"Not really." We couldn't bring him back with us for a proper burial. He'd said the collar was enchanted so that his master could find him, but it was possible that he, too, had been enchanted with a tracking spell.

"Get ready to go," I said to Del as I reached once more for my magic. I didn't want to use it again, but I owed it to him.

My power reached out for Aidan's once more, gathering up the flame. I wished I had a flower or something to put on top of him, but there wasn't time. I released the jet of flame. It struck Aaron's body and enveloped him, reaching high into the night. The damp grass around him would keep the fire from spreading.

My goal had been cremation on a funeral pyre like in a Viking ceremony. I hoped Aaron saw it the same way. My vision was blurry as I took one last look at Aaron, then turned to Del.

"I'm ready." I reached out for her hand.

We crouched down so that we were touching Nix and Aidan. The cathedral glowed in the orange light of the flame. Whoever was coming to meet Aaron would be here soon. Possibly the man from my dreams. Part of me wanted to stay and fight him. Confront him. To have vengeance for Aaron's life and maybe even for what had happened to me and my *deirfiúr*.

But a bigger part of me—the scared, smart part—wanted to run. I would meet this man. The hunter who sought us. But it wouldn't be today.

"We're going," Del said.

I felt her magic pull us through the ether.

CHAPTER FIFTEEN

We appeared at Ancient Magic a moment later. The plywood over the glass windows and door blocked out the sunlight, casting the room in shadow. Or maybe it was just nighttime. I had no idea.

"Call an ambulance," I said to Del, adrenaline still surging through me. "I'll hide the scroll."

I left Del dialing emergency services and headed out the main door. I'd have to stash this stuff in my trove until we found a more secure location. I didn't know why Aaron's master wanted the chalice, but I was hesitant to hand it off to Mr. S. More than likely, it wasn't just a youth charm. I'd have to find him something else to replace it, but I'd worry about that later.

It was dark when I got outside, probably the wee hours after midnight, but that was just a guess. My muscles ached as I took the stairs two at a time up to my apartment and let myself in. The small space looked so familiar, but I felt so different. I could still feel the electricity crackling within me.

Aaron had possessed other gifts—fire and telepathy that he'd used against Del in the fight at Ancient

Magic—but it didn't feel like I'd inherited those. I wasn't entirely sure how it worked, but maybe I'd only taken his root gift. The one he'd been born with. The fire and telepathy had been stolen.

I shook the thought away. I didn't want to think about Aaron or my new powers. It'd take me time to parse through what had happened and how I was going to deal with it and I didn't have the energy. My adrenaline was fading now that I was in the safety of my home.

Quickly, I crossed to the secret door in my bedroom and let myself into my trove. I flicked on the lights and the soothing golden glow reflected off my treasures. Comfort washed over me, followed by bone-aching exhaustion. The only thing that had kept me going had been the adrenaline.

I walked past aisles of my beloved trove. In the back, I dropped to my knees in the corner. With a trembling hand, I pushed aside a pair of boots and pressed my hand to the wall.

My touch ignited the spell that hid the small door. The lock clicked and it swung open. Within, the tiny golden locket glinted from the back corner. It was my only clue about my past.

Or maybe not.

I unzipped the gym bag and pulled out the scroll. It was heavy in my hands. I realized why when I began to unroll it. There had to be twenty feet of rolled vellum here. Quickly, I skimmed it, grateful it was alphabetical and that the monks who had written it had been Irish.

I found FireSouls, and skimmed for our names. When I came upon Cassiopeia Cleraux, Pheonix Knight, and Delphine Hally, my shoulders slumped.

I'd hoped our original names would be written. I didn't know if I'd recognize them, but process of elimination would help. They could have led us to our parents or information about our past.

I ignored the names of the other FireSouls and skimmed the information below our names. Physical descriptions and a list of our powers. I was described as a Mirror Mage, Nix as a Conjurer, and Del as a Transporter and Phantom half-blood.

Whoa. I rocked back on my heels. That was news. I packed the info away for later examination.

I looked for Aaron's name and found it. Lightning Mage. No mention of fire or telepathy abilities. As I'd thought. Stolen powers didn't transfer.

My hands trembled with exhaustion as I rolled up the scroll and put it back in the gym bag. I pushed the bag into the small space and shut the door, then replaced the boots.

By the time I staggered back down to Ancient Magic, Aidan was being loaded into an ambulance. The flashing red and blue lights lit up the night. I ran the last few steps toward the stretcher.

"Ma'am, ma'am! You need to move," a paramedic said.

"I just need to see him," I said, fear tightening my throat. He'd been alive when we'd brought him back to Ancient Magic. He still was, right?

"It's fine," a gravelly voice said from the stretcher.

I nearly collapsed in relief. I'd been operating on instinct to protect my *deirfiúr* and myself when I'd left him at the shop, but now I wanted to see him.

I leaned over the stretcher. His face was wan and his hair singed, but the corner of his mouth kicked up in a smile.

"You don't look so bad, considering you got hit with about a million volts."

"I feel great," he said wryly. "I recommend it."

"I'll keep that in mind."

"Did you get the scroll?" he asked.

My brain blanked. I didn't want to lie to him. I spent my life lying to everyone around me except my *deirfiúr*. For once, I wanted to be honest.

But I couldn't be.

I shook my head and pushed the lie past my tight throat. "No. It was destroyed by the lightning the thief was throwing."

His brow lowered and skepticism flashed on his face. He didn't believe me.

A paramedic hustled up to the other side of the stretcher. "Time to get you to the hospital, Mr. Merrick."

He pushed the stretcher toward the ambulance. I stepped back, grateful for the reprieve.

"You don't need to pay me," I called after Aidan. "I failed, so we're square."

I couldn't hear if he responded. It might not be the last time I saw him, but that was my last word on the matter. As the ambulance pulled away from the curb, I turned toward Ancient Magic.

The lights were on when I entered, casting a harsh glow on the damage that Aaron and his master's demons had caused. Nix and Del sat on the floor, leaning against the counter.

"You look better," I said to Nix.

"I'm conscious and upright, so yeah, I feel better," Nix said.

"They didn't want to take you with Aidan?" I asked.

"I wouldn't let them. He was zapped by a full bolt and was too weak to stop them. I just got knocked out when I touched the side of the cage."

"I told her not to," Del said.

"I never listen," Nix said.

"Aidan will be okay, though, right?"

"Yeah," Nix said. "The paramedics just said they were taking him in for monitoring and rehydrating. They said all his limbs worked and stuff, and he was talking."

"Good." I sank down next to my *deirfiúr* and stared at the wreckage of our shop. "Man, it's been a shitty week."

Del laughed. "Understatement."

"I could eat a horse and sleep for two days." My head dropped back onto the counter behind me.

"Connor and Claire came by when they heard the ambulance. They're coming back with pasties."

"Awesome." I hoped they'd bring a lot.

"Del said you found the scroll. What'd you do with it?" Nix asked.

"Stashed it in my trove, but we need to put it somewhere no one will find it. And that can't be traced back to us."

Nix blew out a breath. "That'll be tough. Can't exactly take out a safety deposit box."

It'd work, if only we could trust the bank not to look in our box. It wasn't a risk I was willing to take.

"So, Del," I said. "That scroll said that you are part Phantom."

"Whoa." Her forehead creased. "I have no idea what that means. Or what to do with that info."

"We'll figure it out," I said.

She sighed. "Yeah."

"Anything about me?" Nix asked.

"Nothing we don't know."

"I guess I'm kinda relieved," she said. "So what happened back there—while I was passed out?" Nix asked.

I heaved out a sigh. Where to start?

Aaron. "The thief who destroyed this place wasn't actually a bad guy."

Nix's head whipped toward me. "What?"

I told them about Aaron and his collar. About how his master was hunting us as well. About how I felt like shit for killing him.

"Man, that sucks," Del said. "You didn't do anything wrong, Cass. It was just a shitty situation. It sounds like he was happy in the end."

"He felt happy. At peace," I said.

"He'd have to be, after what he lived through," Nix said. "How awful, being enslaved by a guy who puts a collar on you that will kill you if removed."

"I think it was worse than that," I said. "Aaron had powers that weren't his own. He was born a Lightning

Mage, but he wasn't born with power over fire or telepathy. He'd killed for those. But his soul was so pure once I'd taken the collar off him, I don't think he would have done it willingly."

"So his master is making super FireSouls? To like, fight or something?" Del shuddered. "Monster."

"I don't know what his goal is. But he's hunting us."

"But he doesn't know where we are, right?" Nix asked.

"I don't think so. There was no one left alive to tell him where we are. I killed every demon who saw us. And Aaron." I rubbed my upper arms, suddenly chilled. "I feel like a monster."

"You did what he wanted," Nix said. "He gave you his power. Willingly. He taught you how to take it. Don't dwell on the bad. Use it to get even. Because the monster is coming for us."

She was right. Logically, I knew it. But I'd killed a man tonight and taken his power. I just didn't know how to process what I'd done. I'd spent my whole life resisting this.

Now my options were to keep ignoring my gifts and disrespect Aaron's last wish—that I use his power to defeat the monster who hunted us—or to embrace them and eventually be discovered and thrown in the Prison for Magical Miscreants.

They were bad options.

But at least they were options.

And like Nix had said—the monster was coming for us.

I had to decide, I just didn't know how.

The door to Ancient Magic opened. I tensed, still on edge, but it was just Claire and Connor.

Connor held up a brown paper sack. "Brought the promised pasties!"

Claire raised a tray of paper coffee cups. "And lattes!"

At the sight of my friends, warmth and gratitude filled me. It'd been a bad night and bad shit was on the horizon. But today was good. My friends and *deirfiúr* were here.

Aidan would live. I wouldn't see him again—at least not past assuring him that the scroll really was destroyed—but at least he was safe.

At least we all were safe.

For now.

CHAPTER SIXTEEN

Two nights later, I sat in the corner at P & P with Nix and Del after another long day cleaning up Ancient Magic. We'd lost about half our stock—months of hunting work for me—but I couldn't be mad at Aaron over the damage. That was all on his master, the man we now called The Monster.

But I was trying not to think of that tonight. We'd swept up the last broken replica and shard of glass, and new windows had been installed that morning. So tomorrow we'd be back to normal. That was worth celebrating. In the morning, I'd set out in search of another youth charm for Mr. S. Del had found reference to an amulet hidden in a temple in Prague.

Connor and Claire had joined us once their only staff member had shown up. Bridget manned the counter some evenings when Connor wanted a break.

"All right," Connor said as he held up his glass of whiskey. "To Ancient Magic. Back on its feet!"

I touched my glass to his, then clinked my way around the circle, careful not to miss anyone. I was so damned glad to be back with my friends, the threat temporarily averted.

"One more," I said after a sip. I raised my glass. "Health and happiness. Because we have them, and we want to keep them."

"Cheers to that," a deep voice said as we clinked our glasses.

I turned. Aidan stood in the doorway, his hands tucked into his pockets. It was suddenly a bit harder to breathe. His dark hair was shiny instead of singed, and his skin was no longer deathly pale. In his t-shirt and jeans, he looked back to normal. Which was to say, damned good.

And also a pain in my ass.

"Hey, Aidan!" Connor said. "Good to see you, man!"

"You're looking better," Nix said. Though she and Del liked Aidan, after the events at the cathedral, we were all on our guard. Because of my memory, someone hunting us had always been at the periphery of our thoughts. But after what had just happened, the threat had become more real. We were all wary.

They still thought he might be able to help us, but he made me nervous. I'd experienced how powerful he was. Aidan was the freaking Origin, not to mention a full Elemental Mage and a healer. He was too powerful. Eventually he was going to sense what I was, especially now that I had Aaron's lightning gift.

"You look like you're feeling better," Nix said. "Not nearly as crispy."

Aidan grinned. He looked so damned handsome that I wanted to curse him. I settled for cursing myself.

"Come, join us," Claire said. "Want a beer or a whiskey?"

Aidan glanced at me. Clearly he was here to talk about the scroll, but I wasn't ready to lie again. So I said nothing. We'd talk, but it'd be better if it were after a drink and some chatting with my friends. If we were all normal and charming, then he'd be more likely to trust me when I lied, right?

Even the thought turned my stomach.

"Whiskey, thanks," Aidan said. He took the seat next to me.

"You all right?" he asked.

"Yeah." I glanced at him quickly, then away.

"So, they sprung you from the hospital, eh?" Connor asked.

"Clean bill of health," Aidan said.

Claire brought him the whiskey and he thanked her. We chatted about the shop being up and running again.

At first, I was uncomfortable. But Aidan fit right in with my friends. I was genuinely wishing I didn't have to blow him off later tonight.

But I had to. Severing contact with him was safest for us all.

"Hey," Aidan's husky voice was soft near my ear. "Can we talk?"

I glanced at him. Better now than later, I figured. Like a band aid. "Yeah."

"Thanks for the drink, Claire and Connor." He set his empty glass on the table. A twenty was tucked beneath it. "It's been good talking to you all, but I've got to run."

"I'm going to walk him out," I said, not making eye contact with anyone.

I followed him to the door. He held it open and I walked through.

"Can we talk at your place?" he asked as he followed me out.

I looked around at the darkened street. I didn't really want to talk about the scroll out here. "Sure. Come on."

"How are you doing?" he asked as we climbed the stairs to my apartment.

"Fine. You know, getting the shop back together." I hated this awkwardness. But I was about to lie to him, so there was really no avoiding it. I let us into my apartment and asked, "You?"

"Great, now that I've recovered from being a lightning rod."

I swallowed hard at the reminder. "You threw yourself in front of that for me." That made it even harder to lie. And much harder to push him away.

"Yeah, seems that I did."

"Why?"

"Felt like a better option than watching you get lit up." His dark gaze met mine, intense enough to burn.

My heart pounded and my breathing stuttered. This was going to be so much more difficult than I'd thought.

"And I knew you wouldn't use your magic to protect yourself," he added.

He was right about that. "Um, thanks for saving me. I'm sorry I didn't get the scroll."

"You're a bad liar."

"No, I'm not." I was a great liar, even when I didn't want to be. "I really am sorry I couldn't get it. It was destroyed by the lightning."

"You don't have to lie to me, Cass."

I really did. I had to lie to everyone who wasn't Nix or Del, no matter how much it exhausted me. "I'm not lying. I am sorry I didn't get it."

"You are lying. And I know why. I know what you are."

My stomach lurched. "A treasure hunting Mirror Mage? Yeah, I told you that."

"No. You're a FireSoul." His gaze was solemn.

The floor felt like it dropped out from under me. Somehow I stayed upright. I even managed an incredulous laugh. "What are you talking about?"

"Don't worry. I won't tell anyone."

My heart pounded as I searched his gaze. Serious and sincere, but I couldn't risk it. "There's nothing to tell. I'm a Mirror Mage. Nothing too exciting there."

"You're exciting, Cass. But not because you're a Mirror Mage. Or even because you're a FireSoul."

"I'm not a FireSoul!"

"I can feel it, Cass. I'm the Origin and a multi-gift Magica. You can't hide something like that from someone as strong as me. At least not for long."

His tone was so certain, his gaze so steady.

"How?" I asked, dread curdling in my stomach.

"I didn't figure it out right away. Your magic felt strong and strange, but I couldn't place it. When you agreed so quickly to help me—without even discussing payment—I was suspicious. It made me wonder if you thought there was something in the scroll about you. I thought you might just be the ArchMage of Mirror Mages. But it didn't feel right."

The ArchMage was the strongest of that particular gift. "I might be. I don't know."

"I'd say it's likely, especially if you practice. But I figured out you were a FireSoul when I saw you right before they put me in the ambulance. I could feel the lightning in you. You took his power."

"I could have borrowed it as a Mirror Mage and not yet released it."

"Maybe, but I knew that wasn't it. You killed him and took his power."

My throat tightened and my eyes blurred. "I didn't want to. I had to."

His gaze softened. "I know. It's why I haven't told anyone what you are. If you intended to steal powers, you'd have done so by now. You'd be full of them. Why was this time different? Why did you have to take his power?"

"How can I trust you?"

"I don't know." His intense gaze locked with mine. "But I want you to."

"Why?"

"Like I said before, I like you."

"I think you're okay, too." Understatement. But at least my tears had dried up before they dropped.

I figured it was better to tell him the truth and try to gain his sympathy. Maybe even his help. "Aaron gave his power to me. To help me defeat the one who hunts us."

"Hunts you?"

"FireSouls." I told him everything I'd learned from Aaron. When I finally trailed off, his gaze was dark with worry.

"You know this means you have to practice your powers, right?" he said.

"I can't! Someone will figure out what I am and alert the Order of the Magica or the Alpha Council. They'll throw me in prison. I'd rot in there." Though the two governmental organizations were separate, they both agreed that FireSouls were a risk. "It's better for me to just keep hiding."

"You know that won't work forever. The monster who hunts you will find you. You've got to be able to fight him when he does." Passion rang in his voice.

My heart pounded. Part of me knew he was right, just as the other part wanted to pretend the last week had never happened.

"You need to learn to use your magic so that you can control it. Maybe even learn to repress it so that other powerful Magica can't sense your arsenal of gifts."

His logic made sense, but it terrified me. To purposefully—frequently—access my magic? It sounded divine. And scary as hell.

"I'll help you," he said. "You can train on my land. There's no one for miles."

"Thanks, but no. This is working for me. The risk isn't worth it."

His face hardened. "I won't accept that. You have to learn to protect yourself. If you don't, I'll report you to the Order."

I stepped backward. "You wouldn't."

"I would. I'm serious about this, Cass. You'd be safer locked up in prison than you are out here, unable to defend yourself. You're scared, so you're fighting it. But you need to face this."

Anger bubbled in my chest. How dare he? I had actually liked this guy? He was threatening me and demanding I make changes I wasn't ready to make.

But he was right.

The monster was coming. And I was afraid. I was so scared that I was curling up in a ball and refusing to face the inevitable.

But the girl who'd run from the monster ten years ago hadn't curled up and died in that cell. She'd broken free. I didn't know how I'd done it, but I had. I'd changed my destiny.

And I had to do it again.

"Fine," I said. I was still pissed at him, but he was right. "I'll learn to use my magic. On your land. But don't get any ideas. I'm not exactly fond of you anymore."

He grinned. "That's fine. I'm fond enough for the both of us. And when you're strong enough to defeat the monster that hunts you, I'll fight by your side."

Strong enough to fight the monster that hunts me.

I really hoped I would be.

THANK YOU FOR READING!

I hoped you liked *Ancient Magic*. Reviews are *so* helpful to authors. I really appreciate all reviews, both positive and negative. If you want to leave one, you can do so at Amazon.

The sequel to *Ancient Magic* will be available soon. If you'd like to know more about the inspiration for the Dragon's Gift series, please read on for the Author's Note.

AUTHOR'S NOTE

Hey, there! I hope you enjoyed reading *Ancient Magic* as much as I enjoyed writing it. In addition to being a writer, I'm also an archaeologist. As a kid, I loved history (because of the fantasy and historic romance novels I read), Indiana Jones, and Laura Croft. When I started writing novels, it was only a matter of time before I applied my love of archaeology and history to my stories.

Hence, Dragon's Gift was born. However, I knew I had a careful line to tread when writing these books. As I'm sure you know, archaeology isn't quite like Indiana Jones (for which I'm both grateful and bitterly disappointed). Sure, it's exciting and full of travel. However, booby-traps are not as common as I expected. Total number of booby-traps I have encountered in my career: zero. Still hoping, though.

When I talk about treading a line with these books, I mean the line between archaeology and treasure hunting. There is a big difference between these two activities. As much as I value artifacts, they are not treasure. Not even the gold artifacts. They are pieces of our history that contain valuable information, and as such, they belong to all of us. Every artifact that is excavated should be properly conserved and stored in a museum so that everyone can have access to our history. No one single person can own history, and I believe very strongly that individuals should not own artifacts. Treasure hunting is the pursuit of artifacts for personal gain.

So why did I make Cass Cleraux a treasure hunter? I'd have loved to call her an archaeologist, but nothing about Cass's work is like archaeology. Archaeology is a very laborious, painstaking process—and it certainly doesn't involve selling artifacts. That wouldn't work for the fast paced, adventurous series that I had planned for Dragon's Gift. Not to mention the fact that dragons are famous for coveting treasure. Considering where Cass got her skills from, it just made sense to call her a treasure hunter. Even though I write urban fantasy, I strive for accuracy. Cass doesn't engage in archaeological practices—therefore, I cannot call her an archaeologist. I also have a duty as an archaeologist to properly represent my field and our goals—namely, to protect and share history. Treasure hunting doesn't do this. One of the biggest battles that archaeology faces today is protecting cultural heritage from thieves.

I debated long and hard about not only what to call Cass, but also about how she would do her job. I wanted it to involve all the cool things we think about when we think about archaeology—namely, the Indiana Jones stuff, whether it's real or not. But I didn't know quite how to do that while still staying within the bounds of my own ethics. I can cut myself and other writers some slack because this is fiction, but I couldn't go too far into smash and grab treasure hunting.

I consulted some of my archaeology colleagues to get their take, which was immensely helpful. Wayne Lusardi, the State Maritime Archaeologist for Michigan, and Douglas Inglis and Veronica Morris, both archaeologists for Interactive Heritage, were immensely helpful with ideas. My biggest problem was figuring out how to have Cass steal artifacts from tombs and then sell them and still sleep at night. Everything I've just said is pretty counter to this, right?

That's where the magic comes in. Cass isn't after the artifacts themselves (she puts them back where she found them, if you recall)—she's after the magic that the artifacts contain. She's more of a magic hunter than a treasure hunter.That solved a big part of my problem. At least she was putting the artifacts back. Though that's not proper archaeology (especially the damage she caused to the first tomb), I could let it pass. At least it's clear that she believes she shouldn't keep the artifact or harm the site. But the SuperNerd in me said, "Well, that magic is part of the artifact's context. It's important to the artifact and shouldn't be removed and sold."

Now *that* was a problem. I couldn't escape my SuperNerd self, so I was in a real conundrum. Fortunately, that's where the immensely intelligent Wayne Lusardi came in. He suggested that the magic could have an expiration date. If the magic wasn't used before it decayed, it could cause huge problems. Think explosions and tornado spells run amok. It could ruin the entire site, not to mention possibly cause injury and death. That would be very bad.

So now you see why Cass Clereaux didn't just steal artifacts to sell them. Not only is selling the magic cooler, it's also better from an ethical standpoint, especially if the magic was going to cause problems in the long run. These aren't perfect solutions—the perfect solution would be sending in a team of archaeologists to carefully record the site and remove the dangerous magic—but that wouldn't be a very fun book. Hopefully this was a good compromise that you enjoyed (and that my old professors don't hang their heads over).

As with my other books, I like to include real historical sites in my novels. In *Ancient Magic*, there were a few places of note. The first was the monks' island in Ireland. That is a real place called the Skellig Michael, part of the Skellig islands off the coast of southwestern Ireland. It's an amazing place and a UNESCO World Heritage Site. The beehive shaped buildings that I described were inhabited by real monks from the end of the first millennium onward.

The other historic site that I included is on the cover of the book. It is Holyrood Abbey in Edinburgh, Scotland. The final battle site on the hidden island is modeled after the abbey. Edinburgh is just too heavily populated to have an epic final battle without humans noticing, so I moved it to a hidden location :-)

I hope you enjoyed the story and will stick with Cass on the rest of her adventure!

ACKNOWLEDGMENTS

The Dragon's Gift series is a product of my two lives: one as an archaeologist and one as a novelist. Combining these two took a bit of work. I'd like to thank my friends, Wayne Lusardi, the State Maritime Archaeologist for Michigan, and Douglas Inglis and Veronica Morris, both archaeologists for Interactive Heritage, for their ideas about how to have a treasure hunter heroine that doesn't conflict too much with archaeology's ethics. The Author's Note contains a bit more about this if you are interested

Thank you, Ben, for everything you've done to support me in this career. Thank you to my dear friend Emily Keane for reading every story I've written and for sharing your great ideas. As always, your comments were amazing. Thank you to Carol Thomas for sharing your thoughts on the book and being amazing inspiration.

Thank you to Jena O'Connor and Lindsey Loucks for various forms of editing. The book is immensely better because of you!

GLOSSARY

Alpha Council - There are two governments that enforce law for supernaturals—the Alpha Council and the Order of the Magica. The Alpha Council governs all shifters. They work cooperatively with Alpha Council when necessary - for example, when capturing FireSouls.

ArchMage - The greatest mage of that particular skill. For example, the ArchMage of Fire Mages. There can also be an ArchWitch or ArchSorcerer.

Blood Sorceress - A type of Magica who can create magic using blood.

Conjurer - A Magica who uses magic to create something from nothing. They cannot create magic, but if there is magic around them, they can put that magic into their conjuration.

Dark Magic - The kind that is meant to harm. It's not necessarily bad, but it often is.

Deirfiúr - Sisters in Irish.

Demons - Often employed to do evil. They live in various hells but can be released upon the earth if you know how to get to them and then get them out. If they are killed on earth, they are sent back to their hell.

Dragon Sense - A FireSoul's ability to find treasure. It is an internal sense pulls them toward what they seek. It is easiest to find gold, but they can find anything or anyone that is valued by someone.

Elemental Mage – A rare type of mage who can manipulate all of the elements.

Enchanted Artifacts – Artifacts can be imbued with magic that lasts after the death of the person who put the magic into the artifact (unlike a spell that has not been put into an artifact—these spells disappear after the Magica's death). But magic is not stable. After a period of time—hundreds or thousands of years depending on the circumstance—the magic will degrade. Eventually, it can go bad and cause many problems.

Fire Mage – A mage who can control fire.

FireSoul - A very rare type of Magica who shares a piece of the dragon's soul. They can locate treasure and steal the gifts (powers) of other supernaturals. With practice, they can manipulate the gifts they steal, becoming the strongest of that gift. They are despised and feared. If they are caught, they are thrown in the Prison of Magical Deviants.

The Great Peace - The most powerful piece of magic ever created. It hides magic from the eyes of humans.

Half-blood - A supernatural who is half one species and half another. Example: shifter and Magica.

Hearth Witch – A Magica who is versed in magic relating to hearth and home. They are often good and potions and protective spells and are also very perceptive when on their own turf.

Magica - Any supernatural who has the power to create magic—witches, sorcerers, mages. All are governed by the Order of the Magica.

Mirror Mage - A Magica who can temporarily borrow the powers of other supernaturals. They can mimick the powers as long as the are near the other supernatural. Or they can hold onto the power, but once they are away from the other supernatural, they can only use it once.

The Origin - The descendent of the original alpha shifter. They are the most powerful shifter and can turn into any species.

Order of Holy Knowledge - A group of monks who collect and protect knowledge that live on an island in Ireland. They are supernaturals, but they do not use their powers.

Order of the Magica - There are two governments that enforce law for supernaturals—the Alpha Council and the Order of the Magica. The Order of the Magica govern all Magica. They work cooperatively with Alpha Council when necessary - for example, when capturing FireSouls.

Phantom - A type of supernatural that is similar to a ghost. They are incorporeal. They feed off the misery and pain of others, forcing them to relive their greatest nightmares and fears. They do not have a fully functioning mind like a human or supernatural. Rather, they are a shadow of their former selves. Half bloods are extraordinarily rare.

Scroll of Truths - A compendium of knowledge about the strongest supernaturals. It is a prophetic scroll that includes information about future powerful beings.

Seeker - A type of supernatural who can find things. FireSouls often pass off their dragon sense as being Seeker power.

Shifter - A supernatural who can turn into an animal. All are governed by the Alpha Council.

Transporter - A type of supernatural who can travel anywhere. Their power is limited and must regenerate after each use.

ABOUT LINSEY

Before becoming a writer, Linsey Hall was a nautical archaeologist who studied shipwrecks from Hawaii and the Yukon to the UK and the Mediterranean. She credits fantasy and historical romances with her love of history and her career as an archaeologist. After a decade of tromping around the globe in search of old bits of stuff that people left lying about, she settled down and started penning her own adventure novels. Her Dragon's Gift series draws upon her love of history and the paranormal elements that she can't help but include.

This is a work of fiction. All reference to events, persons, and locale are used fictitiously, except where documented in historical record. Names, characters, and places are products of the author's imagination, and any resemblance to actual events, locales, or persons, living or dead, is coincidental.

Linsey@LinseyHall.com
www.LinseyHall.com
https://twitter.com/HiLinseyHall
https://www.facebook.com/LinseyHallAuthor

BONNIE
DOON
PRESS

ISBN 978-1-942085-06-5

12-16

1.05.17		

DEMCO 38-301

CPSIA information can be obtained
at www.ICGtesting.com
Printed in the USA
LVOW12s1507140716
496335LV00001B/96/P